THE FEAR OF WINTER

Book One in **THE FEAR OF** Series

S.C. Sterling

N/B Books

Book Design by Charles Layton

Ways to connect with Scott:
www.scsterling.com
sc@scsterling.com

ISBN: 978-0-9970175-2-6

THE FEAR
OF WINTER

Tom released the death grip on the steering wheel, and with his eyes closed, he put the 4Runner in park. Leaning back into the headrest, he listened to his heart pounding against his chest and took a few deep breaths in an attempt to calm his nerves. At almost sixty miles per hour, the collision had been a blur, and he'd had no opportunity to swerve, but that was probably for the best.

He exhaled, then opened his eyes.

The 4Runner had come to a stop at a 30-degree angle, diagonally across the highway and the gravel shoulder. The passenger-side headlight was dark, and the driver-side headlight beamed into the dense forest. Outside, the trees were motionless.

There were no signs of the animal, but judging by the impact, Tom's best guess was that it had been a deer, maybe a fawn. He'd hit an adult male elk as a teenager, and it had collapsed the roof, almost crushing him inside the car. Luckily, this impact wasn't as catastrophic.

Tom pressed the hazard button and turned off the vehicle, then rolled down the window. He listened for a few moments, but the only thing he could hear was his heart.

He stepped out of the car and quietly shut the door. The night was cold against his ears and neck. The temperature was probably in the low twenties, maybe even in the teens. He walked to the front of the 4Runner to survey the damage.

The radiator grille, bumper, and right front fender were caved in, the passenger-side headlight was completely missing, and the "Colorado Native" license plate frame was shattered. Blood was splattered across the hood and fender, and strains of fur were entwined in the plastic cracks.

Tom turned back to the embankment, looking to the east, then west, then back, but there was no sign of the animal.

His head hurt. Probably a concussion from hitting the windshield.

Trudging to the rear of the 4Runner, he opened the hatch, retrieved the roadside emergency kit, and removed a flashlight. He shined the light across the highway and followed the skid marks, which stretched about thirty feet, maybe longer. The smell of rubber still hung in the air.

Tom started back along the embankment, shining the light across the forest. He contemplated driving away, but his conscience wouldn't let him sleep knowing there could be a mortally wounded animal dying at the edge of the forest. Hopefully it had died from the collision or broken its neck on the landing, or run deep into the forest and found a final resting spot to succumb to the injuries. Anything that would keep him from using his gun. He didn't want to kill tonight.

About a tenth of a mile from the crash, Tom stopped in ankle-deep snow.

"No, no, no," he whispered, shaking his head.

The flashlight found the fawn hiding behind the trunk of a Douglas fir about forty feet directly ahead. The animal was curled up in the snow drift—ears back, eyes closed, lying in a pool of blood-soaked snow, gasping for every breath. Tom stood there for a long time, shining the light on the fawn.

Suddenly, the animal sprang up, but almost immediately it dropped back into its own footprint. It looked up at Tom, then slowly turned back to the forest. Defeated, it appeared to accept its impending fate.

Tom was about fifteen steps down the embankment when the roar of an engine broke the silence. He turned back to the highway. Through the trees, he could faintly see the shimmering headlights of a truck. The engine roared louder and louder. It sounded like an eighteen-wheeler, and if the driver was speeding, they'd have little time to react to the back of Tom's 4Runner still parked on the dark and icy road.

Tom ran up the embankment but slipped and fell on his stomach, partially knocking the wind out of him. He pushed to his knees, then jumped up and began high-stepping through the snow.

Upon reaching the pavement, he started a full sprint. About a minute later, he reached the vehicle, climbed in, turned the key, pulled the gear shift into drive, and stepped on the gas. Snow crunched as he steered the car off the highway.

Tom leaned back and fixated on the driver-side mirror. The truck was practically on top of him, and for a moment he thought it might still collide with his car and hurl him into the forest as he had done to the fawn.

The deafening engine rattled the entire vehicle as it passed. After about twenty seconds, it was gone, disappearing into the darkness of Highway 40 and the Rocky Mountains.

Tom turned off the car and stepped outside. He walked back down the highway until he found his tracks. Stopping for a second, he looked up to the night sky. A coyote howled in the distance, but after it faded, there was nothing.

Slowly, he traced the snow tracks down the embankment, moving the flashlight across the forest. His breath was a thick, white cloud.

"Hey boy, where'd you go? Nothing to be afraid of," he said, slowly removing the Glock 17 from his belt.

Halfway down the embankment, Tom spotted the pool of blood in the snow. He stopped and stared. The deer was gone, the forest was still, and Tom was alone.

Wiping the snow out of his eyes, he started back up the embankment as the crescent moon disappeared behind a cloud.

Tom turned off County Road 50 and into his driveway. A light shone from the kitchen, but there was no sign of Lisa. He sat in his car and stared at the house.

After a couple minutes, he opened the door and stepped into a few inches of snow on the driveway. It crunched under his Merrell boots. Tom contemplated shoveling the driveway and walkway right then, but he decided against it. It was too cold, and he was tired. It'd have to wait until tomorrow, or maybe the day after, or maybe the weekend.

At the front of the 4Runner, Tom looked down at the

bumper. He stared at the damage for a moment and then continued up the driveway.

Tom stepped onto the porch, grabbed a handful of salt from a Home Depot bucket, and tossed it on the stairs and walkway. Turning to the front door, he placed his hand on the doorknob and felt it twist. Lisa had left it unlocked again.

He walked in and untied his boots, placing them on the boot tray. The furnace rattled a few times, then smoothed into the calming sound of natural gas. It was hot, probably in the high seventies; Lisa never lowered the thermostat below seventy-five in the winter.

The TV was on but muted, a rerun of *Seinfeld*. A quilt lay half on, half off the couch, and a near-empty wine glass stood atop the coffee table with no coaster. Tom picked up the remote, turned off the TV, then grabbed the wine glass and started to the kitchen. The warped hardwood floor creaked with every step.

A pile of dishes towered in the sink, and an open prescription pill bottle rested on the table. Picking it up, Tom found that it was empty. Xanax, 1mg, Quantity 30, prescribed to Lisa three days ago with the instructions to "Take 1 tablet every 8 hours as needed for anxiety." He stared at it for a minute, maybe longer. This was the fourth empty bottle he'd discovered in the last few weeks: this one, the one on the floor next to her nightstand, the one in the bathroom trash can, and the one in her glove box. In all likelihood, there were many more.

He placed the glass on the counter next to the sink, dropped the pill bottle in the trash, and opened the cupboard, removing a rocks glass. An assortment of whiskey bottles stood on the hutch—Buffalo Trace, Jack Daniel's, Johnnie Walker, Wild Turkey, and Maker's Mark.

Opening the Jack Daniel's bottle, Tom poured a few

shots into the glass and drank it down in two gulps without wincing. He refilled the glass about two thirds of the way, then put the bottle back on the hutch. Sipping on the whiskey, he stared out the kitchen window, watching snowflakes fall to the earth.

A sound came from behind, and Tom turned to the hallway. Max, his eleven-year-old black lab, was standing there, breathing labored, his hind legs shaking.

"Hey boy, you snuck up on me. How are you doing tonight?" Tom said with a smile.

Max had once been a great adventurer and the perfect hiking partner, but now spent the better part of his days sleeping at the foot of the bed. The only time he got up was to eat or go to the bathroom, and more often than not lately he didn't make it outside for that. He was near-blind, probably deaf, and hadn't barked in over a year. Tom knew Max would be lucky to make it another year, and sometimes contemplated taking him out back to put him out of his misery, but he couldn't imagine a day without Max. The dog was currently Tom's only friend and his closest confidant.

"Are you hungry, Maxie?"

Tom grabbed a dog bowl, dumped a cup of Purina into it, then placed it in front of Max. The dog stared at him for a moment, blinking a few times, then bowed down and slowly began to eat. Tom rubbed his head for a bit before walking back to the table, where he resumed sipping on the whiskey. His eyes were heavy as he watched Max bury his nose into the bowl.

A few minutes later, the dog walked over to the table and lay down on the kitchen rug, closing his eyes. Tom bent down and started rubbing his head.

"That's a good boy."

Sometime later, Tom rose and started up the stairs.

Partway down the hallway, he stopped at Megan's room. Tom pushed the door open and peered in. A faint musky smell surrounded him. It had been almost six months since he'd stepped into her room, and it was exactly how he remembered it. Virtually untouched.

Tom carefully walked across the undisturbed carpet to sit at the edge of the perfectly made bed. Running his finger across the gray comforter, he looked up at the ceiling, then closed his eyes. He could almost hear her voice calling for him. Almost.

Rubbing his eyes, he looked around the room. Her dresser, her nightstand with the alarm clock flashing twelve, her desk with textbooks and notebooks and a mini gumball machine, and finally her cork board, with nature pictures, a work schedule, and inspirational quotes tacked onto it.

Out of the corner of his eye, he saw a photo album labeled "More Summer Vacation Pictures" on the bottom shelf of the desk. He reached for it and began turning the pages. Disneyland, Miami Beach, Seattle, Moab, birthday parties, camping, and Yellowstone. Yellowstone was his favorite vacation. They'd gone there for a week when Megan was nine. They made it to almost every major attraction in the park—Old Faithful, Mammoth, Yellowstone Canyon, Grand Prismatic. They even saw a grizzly bear cub in a visitor center parking lot. Megan had named him Freddy.

What he wouldn't give to have one more vacation with her.

Tom shifted on the bed to look out the window but found himself staring at his reflection for a few moments instead. He closed the album, placed it back on the shelf, and got off the bed. After straightening the wrinkles in the comforter, he started toward the door. He turned off the light and blew a kiss, closing the door behind him.

Continuing on to the master bedroom, Tom found that the door was shut.

In front of the dark wooden door, he started to think about his life. All of the mistakes and all of the failures that had brought him to this moment. He considered turning around and walking back downstairs, but after a minute, he gave a light knock.

"Lisa?" he said. No response. After a few seconds, he knocked louder.

"Lisa, are you awake?"

Nothing again. Tom turned the handle and pushed the door open.

Lisa was sitting cross-legged in the middle of the bed, holding an empty wine glass. Her head tilted up slowly, and she stared at Tom as if looking directly through him.

"Are you okay?"

He already knew the answer.

She remained motionless. Finally, she said, "I didn't hear you get home."

"Yeah, I got here about an hour ago. I was feeding Max."

"Oh."

"Have you had dinner? Want me to make you something?"

Lisa looked into the empty wine glass.

"I was at Perks today, just sitting alone, sipping on a coffee, reading the paper, and a group of three women sat down at the table directly behind me. I'd never seen them before, and I doubt they recognized me."

Lisa started flicking her index finger against the glass.

"They were discussing how bored they were with their husbands, and their families and their lives. Just the mundane bullshit I always overhear women talk about, nothing captivating. But then the topic changed. They started talking about the Bob Anderson murder and the murder of some nurse in Boulder a few years ago, and a couple of hitchhikers who were murdered on Hoosier Pass back in the eighties. They were fucking giddy the way they talked about it. It was disgusting, and I was about to get up—then one of them mentioned Megan's name. I leaned back to get a better listen."

"Why, Lisa?"

"The fat one said they heard a rumor that Megan was abducted, raped for a few days, then tied to a tree and left for dead. Either dead from the elements or wildlife or the killer sliced her throat."

"You know that's just stupid small-town gossip," Tom said.

She shook her head. "How do you know that? You've been looking for almost two years, and you're not any closer to finding her than the day she vanished. And I'm sitting here living my own fucking nightmare. Every waking moment. I can't touch her, hug her, kiss her, or even bury her. She isn't alive and she isn't dead—she's a lost soul in some fucking purgatory."

"I'm going to find her," Tom said, choking on his words.

Deep down, in places he was scared to visit, he knew that Megan might never be found, but he could never utter those words, especially to Lisa.

"I hope you're prepared to find a scattered pile of bones."

He didn't answer.

"You couldn't find the killer of those kids, and you're not going to find Megan!"

Before his own daughter's tragedy, not solving the murder of the kids in the pizzeria was his biggest failure.

"Please stop."

She looked up at Tom and without warning threw the wine glass at the closet door. It shattered, and hundreds of tiny shards fell to the carpet. Neither of them flinched; their eyes remained locked.

"I hate you for convincing me to move here. I really do. I wish I would've said no. If I had, Megan would still be alive."

"She is not dead, and I promise that I won't stop looking until I find her."

"Let me give you a piece of advice. She is never coming back. Never. Megan is dead. She's gone forever."

"I love you, but you're wrong."

"Then where the fuck is she?" Lisa screamed, spitting the words.

"I don't know," Tom whispered.

ONE

Tom sat alone in the back booth of Rocky Mountain Café, a diner with a capacity of around thirty in downtown Granby. Conversations meshed into one loud, incoherent, ambient noise, and the sound of silverware against glass plates and cups echoed throughout the room. The smell of bacon grease seeped from the walls. A small white storage box with "MEGAN" written on the lid sat in the booth next to Tom.

He took the final drag off his cigarette, then smashed the butt into the ashtray. Flipping through the *Rocky Mountain News*, he glanced at each headline before moving to the next story: "Teen Fires on Classmates – 8 Killed, 5 Wounded in Kentucky High School Shooting"; "Details Pointing to Nichols, Government's Case Solid in Oklahoma City Bombing, Experts Say"; "Denver Council Backs Needle Exchange."

Tom closed the paper and slid it across the table. He looked at his watch then over his shoulder to the front door. Recognizing the owner of County Hardware five booths down, he gave a courtesy wave. He couldn't remember the man's name—something with a *b*. Bob, or maybe Bill. He'd always been bad with names.

He tore open a sugar packet, then dumped the granules into the stained white porcelain coffee cup. After a few sips, he pulled a binder out of the box and started reading the pages, instantly becoming oblivious to everyone and everything in the diner.

Sometime later a voice said, "Tom Floyd?"

Tom looked up from the binder and extended his arm for a handshake. "Yes, and you must be Marshall. It's nice to finally meet you in person. And thanks for making the drive up here."

"Likewise, and no problem. I'll take any excuse to get out of the city."

Marshall removed his overcoat, laid it in the booth, and dropped a notepad on the table.

A waitress stealthily approached. "What can I get you, sugar?"

"I'll take a coffee." He picked up the menu and swiftly skimmed it. "And give me the Rocky Mountain Breakfast—over easy, bacon, and white toast."

"You got it. Anything else for you, Tom?" she said.

"I'm good with the coffee, thanks."

"Sounds good. I'll be right back," the waitress said with a smile.

Tom slid the binder toward the wall and picked up the cup, taking another sip before addressing Marshall. "I've never been impressed by those fancy coffee shops—give me a coffee with some cream and a couple packets of sugar from a place like this any day of the week."

The alarm clock buzzed, and Hannah slammed her palm onto the snooze button. She slowly opened one eye and squinted at the digital display—9:17.

"Fuck," she groaned.

Meticulously she climbed out of the covers so as not to disturb her American Shorthair cat, Milo. Standing next to her bed she stretched her arms to the stucco ceiling while yawning. Hannah caught a glimpse of herself in the full-length mirror propped against the wall and quickly turned away. The sight of the countless scars on her inner thighs gave her a conflicted feeling. She knew the cutting wasn't healthy, but it was euphoric.

Self-mutilation was something she'd discovered a few months after her nineteenth birthday. That first cut against her right thigh was a moment she'd never forget, like losing your virginity. Removing the blade from her dresser drawer, placing the cold metal against her flesh, pressing down then slowly pulling it up, and the sensation of trickling blood.

It was small, a surface cut, only a quarter of an inch deep and an inch long. But it was enough. She'd been numb to life for years and instantly felt alive. Soon she was going deeper, and longer. Two, three, four, five cuts in a single session. Once, she attempted to count the number of scars but stopped after fifty.

Hannah craved the feeling more than anything, like a heroin addict searching for the next fix, and was scared the urge would never go away.

It'd been sixty-one days since she made a four-inch cut that took over an hour to stop bleeding and completely clot. That one scared her enough to go cold turkey. She couldn't remember the last time she'd made it a month, let alone two.

Bending down, she grabbed a pair of pants off the floor then slipped on an oversized Guns N' Roses Use Your Illusion Tour T-shirt.

Hannah walked into the kitchen, opened the refrigerator, and grabbed a near-empty half-gallon of whole milk and a box of Cinnamon Toast Crunch off the counter.

Taking a seat at the kitchen table, she turned on the TV, flipping channels aimlessly with almost every bite before finally stopping on *The Jerry Springer Show*. The episode was about a mother who was sleeping with her daughter's boyfriend.

Hannah finished, slurped the remaining milk, then placed the bowl in the sink on top of a pile of dishes. She opened a can of Fancy Feast and dumped the clump of meat and liquid mush onto a salad plate. Then she set it on the floor and called for Milo. The cat was in the kitchen within twenty seconds.

In the vase on the kitchen windowsill, the purple lily bouquet was nearly dead—she probably should have thrown it out days ago. It was hard for her to throw them away because purple was her sister's favorite color.

Reluctantly, Hannah grabbed the vase, poured the water down the drain, then threw the flowers in the trash can. Placing the vase on the windowsill, she sat back down, watching Milo eat breakfast.

A knock came at the front door, but Hannah ignored it. Another knock sounded a few seconds later, a little louder. After the fourth series of knocks, she got up and walked to the door.

"Hello Alan," she said, annoyed.

"I heard your TV and figured you were up and thought you might want a cup of Joe," Alan said, holding out a coffee mug.

"Gotta love these paper-thin walls."

He smiled. "Cream and a little sugar?"

She nodded, grabbed the cup, and thanked him.

"And I still would love to take you to dinner sometime. I'm open any night that works for you," he said.

"And for the tenth time, I'm flattered, but like I said the first nine times, I'm going to have to decline," Hannah said.

"I was hopeful the tenth time would be a charm. You can't blame a guy for trying."

"Alan, you're a nice guy and need a good, wholesome girl you can take home to your parents. I can promise you, I'm not that girl."

"And why do you say that?"

"Because I'm fucking crazy," Hannah said.

She thanked him again, then closed the door and sat at the table, staring out the window and sipping on the coffee. Sixty-one days.

After a large drink Tom said, "Fraser is one of the coldest towns in the Lower 48, with supposedly the coldest winters. Back in the fifties, town officials got into a legal dispute with some town in Minnesota over trademarking 'Icebox of the Nation.' The two towns went back and forth for decades over who got the naming rights. It finally got settled when Fraser agreed to relinquish the name in exchange for two thousand dollars. They fought for decades and gave it away for a measly two grand."

Marshall dropped his fork onto the plate, then slid the plate to the edge of the table. He took a drink of coffee before looking up at Tom.

"Did you ask me to drive all the way up here to discuss the local climate and your coffee preferences, or would you like to discuss your missing daughter? I'd prefer to talk about Megan, but if you want to talk about random bullshit, that's your decision. I'm getting paid either way, so it's up to you."

Tom knew Marshall was probably his best and last chance of finding Megan, and that scared him.

"Sorry. It kills me to talk about her, so sometimes I just ramble about nonsense."

"I understand, but if you want me to help, we're going to have to start somewhere."

"What do you want to know?"

"Everything," Marshall said, opening the notepad.

"Okay," Tom said, looking out the window. He wiped his mouth with the back of his hand. "She is our only child. She was nineteen when she went missing, and is going to turn twenty-two in a couple weeks. Her birthday is December 21, a Christmas baby. She hated having her birthday so close to the holiday and would throw a fit about not having separate presents, so we always planned a separate birthday party the weekend before Christmas."

Tom half smiled. He told Marshall about their decision to move because they thought Denver was getting too dangerous, and that Megan was pissed that they'd moved her away from her friends right before she started high school.

"She didn't talk to us for almost a week. I thought it was just a teenager going through a phase, and after she started at the new school she'd have a new group of friends, but she didn't. She had some friends, but I don't think she ever found a best friend up here. I guess you could say she was socially withdrawn from her peers, and the small social circle she did have felt more like acquaintances, except for her boyfriend Jack Gardner."

Tom picked up his coffee but set it back down without taking a drink.

"They started dating during her junior year, and to our knowledge it was her first real boyfriend. He was a nice kid—quiet, polite, came from a good family."

That was the first time Tom could remember seeing her happy since moving to Granby.

"Her and Jack were pretty much inseparable. They both loved the outdoors. They hiked, camped, fished and skied. After graduating, they planned this huge two-week road trip. Moab, Capitol Reef, Zion, Las Vegas, and ending up in Los Angeles. I thought they were going to be together for years, but something happened on that trip, because when she got home, she was a different person, withdrawn and depressed. She finally told us they'd broken up and she didn't want to talk about it, and she never did, to me or Lisa."

He sighed. "She left for CU a couple weeks later, but only lasted that first semester." Tom suspected Jack was the reason why she quit school.

"I told her if she wasn't going to school, she'd have to get a job and pay rent. I really thought that would motivate her to go back, but it didn't. A week later, she got a job at Fraser Market and worked there until the day she disappeared." Tom paused for a moment. "I wish I would've fought for her to stay in school."

Marshall stopped writing and looked up, "Tell me about the day she disappeared."

"Thursday, December 12, 1996. I was eating breakfast, and Megan came downstairs, seemingly in good spirits. She poured a bowl of cereal and sat at the table with me. That was a rare occurrence; most days she'd skip breakfast and say goodbye from the hallway." Tom tapped on the table with his thumb. "I asked about work, and she told me it was good, but she wanted a change. She was going to start looking for a job down in Denver in January. I asked what she wanted to do, and she wasn't sure. I asked if it was because of a boy, and she said no. When I asked what she wanted for her birthday, she just shrugged her shoulders."

"Not much of a talker?" Marshall said.

Tom shook his head. "Then she told me she had to run some errands before work and she'd see me later. I told her I loved her, and she said, 'Bye, Dad' and walked out the door. That was the last time I saw her."

Grand County was massive, spanning over 1,800 square miles of mostly mountainous terrain. The county had six National Wilderness areas, two National Forests, and one National Park—Rocky Mountain. To the west was the Continental Divide and Trail Ridge Road, the highest paved mountain pass in the United States. The land was beautiful, but unforgiving. And despite its size, the county was sparsely populated, with under ten thousand residents. Hot Sulphur Springs, the county seat, had a population of less than five hundred. There were countless places to get lost, or bury a body.

At any given time, there were at least two dozen missing people in the county, mostly hikers or backcountry skiers who were lost to an avalanche. But there were missing people who mysteriously vanished, like Megan. Another tally to the county statistic.

"What time was that?" Marshall asked, scribbling notes again.

"8:45."

"And where'd Megan go after she left your house?"

"She got gas at the Conoco on Fifth Street about fifteen minutes after leaving home. There's CCTV footage—it's grainy, but definitely her. She's alone, and the surrounding pumps were empty. She fueled up, climbed into her car, and turned west onto Highway 40.

Tom opened the binder and removed three low-resolution pictures, sliding them across the table. Marshall studied the pixelated images of Megan pumping gas. Tom avoided looking at them. They always gave him a haunted feeling.

"I'll need a copy of that video."

Tom nodded. "The next time she's seen is between 11:15 and 11:30 at the Outlet Mall in Silverthorne. Three different witnesses saw Megan at the mall: one in the Nike Store, one in the parking lot, and another on the bike path behind the stores. They all stated she appeared to be alone."

"No video?"

"No. Either the stores didn't have them, or they weren't working, or Megan stayed out of view."

"Any receipts, or credit card transactions?"

"She didn't have a credit card, and we never found any record of her making a purchase."

"How long does it take to get from Granby to Silverthorne?"

"An hour and fifteen, maybe on a good day you can do it closer to an hour."

"What route would she most likely take?"

"The fastest way is west on 40 to Kremmling, then south on Highway 9. It's about sixty miles." Tom had probably driven that route thirty or forty times since Megan vanished.

"Do you find it strange she would've driven over an hour to a mall just to window shop?" Marshall asked.

"I know she was saving money, but it does seem out of character for her to drive all the way to Silverthorne and not buy anything."

"Could she have been meeting someone there?"

"Possibly, but I didn't find any evidence that she was."

"Okay. Where does she go after the mall?"

"Work. She arrives at 2:50, ten minutes before her shift."

"In Fraser?" Marshall said.

Tom nodded.

"How long is the drive from the mall to her work?"

"About an hour and twenty minutes."

Marshall tapped the pen on the table. "Would she have gone back up Highway 9 to 40?"

"No, driving up through Granby adds about twenty unnecessary miles. The fastest route is east on I-70 through the tunnel, then north on 40 over Berthoud Pass, about an hour and twenty minutes."

"So, she basically did a big circle from Granby to Silverthorne to Winter Park?"

"Yes, pretty much. About a 125-mile round trip."

"To window shop at an outlet mall?" Marshall said.

"Yes."

"How was the weather?"

"It was a beautiful December Colorado day—clear skies, highs in the low forties."

Marshall stared at the notepad for a few moments. "And she worked at the grocery store in Fraser?"

"Yeah, the Fraser Market. It's a family-owned store that's been in town since the seventies. It's small, but it has a meat department and a decent produce selection. They have anywhere from fifteen to twenty employees, mostly part-timers in their teens or early twenties. Ski bums, students, stoners."

"Any of the employees have any type of criminal record?"

"Minor stuff—MIPs, marijuana possession, trespassing, a couple DUIs."

"Did she have any disputes with any coworkers? Customers?"

"No. The owners said she was well liked by everyone. Her managers said she was amazing, everyone loved her. She didn't have a single complaint in the ten months she worked there."

"And what about her shift that day?" Marshall said.

Tom remembered every detail by heart, like an actor in a Broadway play. Megan had clocked in at 2:58 and worked register two for her entire shift. She'd completed forty-four transactions—twenty-seven by credit card, seven checks, and ten in cash. The last transaction was at 8:25 by Jim Wells, a sixty-eight-year-old retired English teacher who purchased a loaf of bread, a can of Copenhagen, and a pint of vanilla ice cream.

Tom had interviewed Jim twice and was confident he wasn't involved.

"What about the customers who used credit cards and checks?" Marshall asked.

"Yeah, nothing. All locals."

"Does the store have video?" Marshall said.

"Yes, cameras over every register, two pointed at the inside entrance, and one at the loading dock. Nothing in the parking lot."

"I'll need a copy of those as well."

"Of course."

Tom knew it was pointless. He'd watched those videos hundreds of times, and there weren't any clues.

"And what happened after Jim made his purchase?"

"The store closed at 9:00. She counted the drawer, cleaned the register, and clocked out at 9:18. She said goodnight to a few coworkers, then walked out at 9:21."

"Did anyone see her after she left the store?"

"Yeah, a mom who was waiting to pick up her daughter, another cashier there. She was parked toward the front of the parking lot for roughly twenty minutes and didn't see anyone until Megan walked out of the store. She said when Megan walked past her car, they waved to each other. Then a couple minutes later, Megan drove away and turned north onto Highway 40."

"And she was the last person to see Megan?" Marshall said.

Tom nodded.

"Did you expect her home that night?"

"No. It wasn't out of the ordinary for her not to come home after work. Sometimes she'd be gone for a couple days then come home, shower, do laundry, and be gone for another few days. It bothered us, but we knew she was trying to figure her life out, so we gave her space."

"When did you realize she was missing?"

A plate hit the floor and shattered—they both looked to the kitchen for a few moments, then turned back.

"I received a call from her manager at 4:22 the next day, the thirteenth, and he told me Megan didn't show up for her shift. She was never late and had never done a no-call, no-show. I initially thought she had her days off mixed up or something."

"What did you do after that call?"

"I called a few of her friends, but none of them had seen her, or even talked to her in months. That's when I really started to get concerned." Tom cleared his throat. "I called two guys on patrol that day, and they began an unofficial search, and Lisa and I did our own search from Granby to Fraser. There wasn't any sign of her. Nothing." He trailed off on the final word, lost in thought. It took him a moment to start talking again. "We filed the official missing person report a little after ten that night, and by the next morning, there was a search party of almost a hundred people—cops, search and rescue, neighbors and volunteers. They searched by car, by foot, on horseback,

ATVs, hikers in the backcountry, and a tracking dog. There was even a guy who volunteered his Cessna to do an aerial search. Fliers were hung up in what felt like every gas station, grocery store, liquor store, post office, and trailhead in Grand County. All the Denver TV stations did a segment on the ten-o'clock news, and a reporter from the *Denver Post* wrote a feature about it."

"I remember seeing it on Channel 4," Marshall said, not looking up from the notepad.

"Watching everyone come together gave me confidence that Megan would be found, but Saturday turned into Sunday into Monday. Then on Tuesday morning, a storm rolled in and dumped about eight inches. Temperatures dropped to the low teens. That pretty much incapacitated the search, and it felt like each following day, the search party continued to dwindle. By the third week, it was down to four people, and after a month I was the only one left."

"Have there been any other organized searches?"

Tom nodded. "In June, divers searched a section of Will Creek Reservoir. There was a tip about her car being in the lake. I, umm, parked on the road and just watched them go in and out of the water for hours."

That was the worst day of his life, and he'd give anything to get the images of the divers out of his head. For months, every time he closed his eyes, he'd see the divers submerge into the water.

"We can take a break if you want," Marshall said.

"No, I'm okay. Let's keep going."

"Do you have any other leads?"

"No, it's been pretty slim. There was an anonymous call that a guy who owned a cabin and some property outside of Idaho Springs was involved. We questioned him. He was cooperative and had a solid alibi. Then last summer, some hikers stumbled across a decomposing body about twenty feet off a trail while taking a piss on Morse Mountain. I was really optimistic it was Megan."

He instantly realized he'd never said those words aloud—that he was hopeful that a rotting corpse deep in the forest was his baby girl. The thought had crossed his mind countless times, but to speak it so nonchalantly made his stomach turn, and he swallowed audibly.

"But the dental records identified the remains as a twenty-three year-old girl from Denver who didn't return home after a day hike a few years back. It's been ruled accidental. She probably got lost and died of exposure."

"How would you consider your relationship with Megan?"

Tom started to speak, then quickly stopped, thinking about the question.

"Growing up, we were really close—dinners, Broncos games, movies, skiing, camping—but as she got older, she became less interested in spending time with me, and it pretty much stopped when she started dating Jack. I really tried to be involved in her life, but she became very distant that last year."

"Do you think she kept secrets from you?"

"What teenager doesn't keep secrets from their dad?"

"What about your wife?"

"Lisa knew about as much as I did about Megan's life."

"Tell me about her ex, Jack," Marshall said.

"Grew up outside of Tabernash in an upper-middle-class family with two younger siblings. Parents still married, dad is a high-end real estate agent and mom is a nurse. Clean record, not even a speeding ticket. From all accounts, it seems like he's a pretty good kid. He was living in Boulder when Megan went missing, a freshman at CU majoring in Engineering."

"Was he ever considered a suspect?"

"Yes, briefly. And he lawyered up within a few days, but he cooperated with the investigation and passed a polygraph. After that, he was no longer considered a suspect."

"Do you think he could've been involved?"

Tom scratched his beard. "I honestly don't know. I go back and forth about him, but at the end of the day, I don't think it was him."

"Do you have any other suspects?"

Tom paused momentarily, then slowly said, "Kevin Strand."

"The Rocky Mountain Killer?"

Barely audible Kevin sang the second verse of "Good Vibrations" by The Beach Boys while drumming along on the steering wheel. His eyes remained focused on the flashing lights in the rearview mirror. After a few minutes, the door to the Colorado State Patrol car opened, and the trooper started approaching his vehicle.

Kevin ejected the cassette, then rolled down the window. Leaning back, he waited patiently.

The trooper shined a flashlight in Kevin's face for a couple seconds, then aimed it at the passenger seat, then the backseat, then back to Kevin.

"Where are you heading?"

"Home. I just got off work," Kevin said.

"Where's home?"

"Off Highway 9 south of Kremmling."

"Have you had anything to drink tonight?"

"No sir, I never touch the stuff."

"Good for you. Can I get your license, insurance, and registration?"

"Yes sir."

Kevin removed his license from his wallet, then rummaged through documents and maps in the glovebox until he found his insurance and registration. He handed them to the trooper.

"Please sit tight for a few minutes."

Kevin watched the man walk back to his patrol car in the rearview mirror.

"You are doing so good," Kevin whispered. "And if you stay quiet, I won't make this any worse than it has to be."

He started humming the melody of "Good Vibrations", watching cars drive by, oblivious to the situation.

Ten minutes later, the officer returned. "Do you know why I pulled you over?"

"I don't."

"Your passenger-side taillight is out."

"Really? I had no idea," Kevin said, turning back to look.

"I'm going to let you off with a warning tonight, but if I see you again and that light isn't fixed, I'll have to issue you a ticket."

"Thank you very much, and I'll get it fixed first thing tomorrow."

"Have a good night and drive safe," the trooper said as he walked away.

"You as well. God bless."

Kevin rolled up the window and watched the patrol car drive toward the horizon and out of sight. When he was confident it was gone, he stepped out of the car and made his way back to the trunk. He delicately slid his hand across the metal.

"You were so good," Kevin whispered.

He slid the key into the lock and turned it. The trunk popped open, and he stared down at the girl, who lay motionless on the carpet.

Terror was seared into her eyes. Her hands and feet were bound with zip ties, and her mouth was covered with duct tape. Kevin put his hand on hers, and she squirmed.

"Nothing to worry about, sweetie, it's only me," he said while caressing her soft hair.

The girl tried to yell, but it was muffled. Her eyes were bulging.

"I'm sorry, sweetie, but it's just me and you. No one can help you now. No one." Kevin leaned into the trunk and hovered over her. "I promise you, this will all be over soon."

He slammed the trunk, got back in the car, put it in drive, and pulled onto Highway 40.

Kevin Strand was Colorado's second most notorious serial killer only behind Ted Bundy. Six confirmed victims, and some speculated the number could have been closer to twelve or fifteen. All the victims were abducted in Grand County, mutilated, burned in a steel drum, then scattered on his four-acre property outside of Kremmling. Almost two dozen forensic scientists and members of the Colorado Bureau of Investigation had spent ten days searching the property, and the largest human remains they found was the left foot of his first victim, Diane Moore.

Diane had been a nineteen-year-old vagabond, traveling cross country attempting to hike every National Park in the Lower 48. She was hitchhiking outside of Grand Lake, holding a cardboard sign with "MOAB" written in big, black letters when Kevin pulled onto the shoulder and offered her a ride. They made small talk, flirted a little, then twenty minutes after picking up Diane, he hit her in the head with a pipe wretch. He pushed her onto the floorboard, covered her with a blanket, and continued home. She'd be dead within hours.

Kevin wasn't sure why he killed Diane—he'd picked up countless hitchhikers over the years and never had the urge to harm anyone until he looked into her eyes. It was at that moment he knew Diane would never leave his presence. He was only twenty-four, and he wouldn't have the urge again for another five years.

The murders that made him infamous, the ones that spawned the Rocky Mountain Killer nickname and the made-for-TV movie starring Charlie Sheen, were the mother, Sharon, and her two teenage daughters, Rebecca and Julie.

Sharon was recently divorced, and taking her daughters on a much-needed vacation before the start of school. A Southwest road trip—the Grand Canyon, four nights in a houseboat on Lake Powell, visiting family in Denver, and a weekend in Grand Lake before driving home to Las Vegas.

They were staying at the Bear Lake Lodge, a few miles outside of Rocky Mountain National Park, where Kevin worked as a handyman. He met Rebecca at the vending machine and gave her directions to popular area hikes.

A little after midnight, he used the hotel master key to gain access to their room while they were sleeping and forced them to tie each other up at gunpoint. One by one, he wrapped them in a blanket, flung them over his shoulder, and carried them out to his work van. Two hours later, they were on his basement cement, and all of them were dead before sunrise.

He murdered two more women before being apprehended: Amy, a National Parks volunteer studying geology, and Laura, a part-time barista.

After his capture, he provided investigators with

meticulous details of all six murders. And in exchange for a guilty plea, he asked for the death penalty. The judge granted the request, and on the one-year anniversary of his final murder, Kevin was sentenced to death by way of lethal injection.

He'd spend his final days in solitary confinement, and unlike Ted Bundy, he'd never escape from a Colorado prison.

"Isn't his execution date this summer?" Marshall said.

"Yeah, July." Tom nodded. "He's waived all appeals and is asking for an expedited execution date. He wants to die."

"And I assume he's been asked about Megan."

"Yes. Investigators interrogated him over a two-day period about unsolved murders and disappearances in Colorado, Wyoming, and Utah. He only admitted to the six murders," Tom said.

"And what makes you think he might be involved with Megan?"

"He abducted the last girl about fifty minutes from our house. He was a regular at all the bars around Fraser. There are credit transactions at the Fraser Market during the same time Megan worked there."

"So, all circumstantial?"

Tom turned away. He knew Kevin was a longshot—a 1980s US Hockey Team to win the gold type of longshot.

Marshall looked down at the notepad a final time, then closed it and dropped his pen on the cover. "What do you really think happened?"

"As a father, I pray she just packed up and ran away to start a new life, and one day I'll open the door and she'll be standing on my porch. As a cop, statistics say she probably was dead within twenty-four hours." Tom picked up the storage box and placed it on the table. "Here is everything you should need. List of friends, coworkers, classmates, phone numbers, bank statements, pay stubs, concert tickets, pictures, yearbooks, work schedules, and a copy of her journal. Megan's entire life in a box." He cleared his throat. "I know I'm probably never going to see her smile or hear her voice or see her do her stupid dance, and that kills me. But I have to know what happened. I need fucking closure, and you're my last chance at that."

Megan was officially a cold case, and outside of dumb luck, like hikers stumbling upon the body, Tom knew if Marshall failed, Megan would probably never be found.

Hovering over a rusted metal drum, Kevin studied the flames dance above the rim. Clouds of heavy black smoke billowed to the east toward the countless mountain peaks behind him. After a long moment he began circling the drum. It was single digits, and without the fire, Kevin could succumb to hypothermia in under an hour.

He stopped, then turned back to his house and listened for a minute, maybe two. He'd thought he heard something, but now there was nothing.

Removing the purse from his shoulder, he opened it. A set of keys, a wallet, red lipstick, eyeliner, four tampons, and a brush. Kevin removed the keys and slipped them into his coat pocket. Then he placed the comb under his nose and inhaled. The smell reminded him of her. He ran it through his hair a few times before putting it back into the purse.

When he dropped the purse in the fire, the fire came alive. Kevin was hypnotized by the flames. He stood there for a long time, licking his lips and tasting the metallic air.

As he wiped the sweat off his forehead, he noticed blood on his palm. Bending down, he grabbed a handful of snow, then started rubbing his hands together, dissolving the snow into water and diluting the blood until they were clean. He stared at his hands for a long moment, then dried them on the front of his flannel.

Kevin turned back to the house as the sun was breaking over the mountains. It'd been a long night, and he was tired. It was time for sleep.

TWO

L eaning back into the couch Marshall stared into the empty dining room. He'd never bothered to replace the kitchen table. What was the point? After the divorce, there had only been a handful of visitors, and he couldn't remember anyone who'd been there in the last year. And when he did eat, it was usually standing at the counter or over the sink.

He'd offered the house to Cheryl during the divorce procedures, but she declined, only wanting the car, the kitchen table, and a few small appliances. Over the years, he'd considered putting it on the market, but once he moved out, that'd be the final tie to his previous life, his normal life, his happy life. And as sad as it was to live here alone, it'd be worse not to have the memories. The house was his memento.

Within a few hours of the judge signing the divorce papers, Cheryl had the car packed up and was heading to Arizona, taking Sara, his only child, with her. He wanted to fight for custody, but he knew he didn't stand a chance.

Cheryl was a saint, a third-grade teacher with a contagious smile who'd never had as much a speeding ticket, and he was an unfaithful, alcoholic cop with an assault charge for a domestic dispute.

The domestic charge still haunted him. He came home drunk and Cheryl cornered him, accusing him of cheating, and in an attempt to get away, he inadvertently knocked her to the hardwood floor, shattering her left wrist. Sara ran out of the bedroom and saw her mother in agony and looked up at Marshall with disgust.

Cheryl went to the emergency room, Sara went to her grandma's, and Marshall spent the next two days in Jefferson County Jail. He'd arrested dozens of men for domestic violence, and always thought how pathetic they were for hitting a woman, and now he was one of them.

And even though it was an accident and he never intended to hurt Cheryl, he knew that didn't matter. There was nothing he could say or do to fix the marriage. It was over. Cheryl asked for a divorce and full custody, and he agreed. She told him they were moving to Arizona, and all he did was silently nod.

It'd been over five years since he'd spoken to Sara, and last he heard she was attending Arizona State. He'd sent a birthday card in August, but hadn't received a response. He didn't expect one. Odds were she threw it in the trash when she saw the return address. Sara hated him, and he didn't blame her.

Marshall emptied a bottle of Valium onto his kitchen table and moved the blue pills around like casino chips. Placing one pill in front of him, he picked up a lighter and worked the pill until it was nothing but a fine powder. Then he rolled up a five-dollar bill and snorted it.

Near comatose, he stared out the kitchen window, thinking about his life, his mistakes and regrets. After a few minutes, he reached across the table for the cordless phone and dialed Hannah's number.

Hannah hung up the phone, then walked over to the four-foot-tall, five-shelf CD rack. The rack held 230 CDs, all sorted in alphabetical order, with overflow stacked about ten high on the floor on either side of the rack. Most of the albums were alternative, grunge, and rock— Radiohead, Nirvana, Smashing Pumpkins, Beastie Boys, Pixies, Nine Inch Nails, Jawbreaker. There was some classic rock as well: Pink Floyd, The Rolling Stones, David Bowie, and The Clash.

She hated the silence, so music was always playing or the TV was always on. Background noise was a tool to help control her thoughts. Being alone in her head was a scary place.

Running her finger down the CD case spines, she searched for the evening soundtrack. She stopped in the middle of the fourth shelf and removed a case—*Siamese Dream* by The Smashing Pumpkins. She slid the CD into the Discman, closed the lid, and pressed play. The disc began to spin, then after a few seconds of silence, a quick snare roll signified the start of "Cherub Rock." The snare was followed by a clean guitar, then bass quarter notes, and finally the distorted guitars. It gave her chills every time. Hannah smiled—her favorite song on her current favorite album.

Favorite albums usually only lasted a week or two, and on the rare occasion only a couple of days. Last week it was *In Utero* by Nirvana, and before that it was Pink Floyd, *Wish You Were Here*, Oasis, *(What's the Story) Morning Glory?*, and Guns N' Roses, *Appetite for Destruction*, with *The Bends* by Radiohead making an appearance almost quarterly. Hannah could lie in the middle of the floor and listen to "High and Dry" or "Fake Plastic Trees" on repeat for hours. That was her sanctuary.

For some people, music could be life-changing; for Hannah, it was lifesaving. At certain times in her life, music had been her only friend, and she felt closer to a musician she'd never met than someone she'd talked to hundreds of times. That was by choice, though. For Hannah, it was easier to push people away than get close to someone.

She grabbed her coat, slipped the Discman into her purse, and stepped out of her apartment. After slamming the door, she walked five steps, then suddenly stopped. Turning around, she stared at the doorknob. She knew she'd locked it, but the longer she stared, the more uncertain she became. Hannah hated this feeling, but as the thoughts became routine, she became accustomed to them and accepted them. Finally, after twenty seconds, she walked over to the door and placed her hand on the doorknob. The door was locked, but she turned it three more times, silently counting with each turn.

In the alley outside her building, the aroma of piss punched her in the face, but it quickly faded. She was used to the smell, and it was a prerequisite of living in Capital Hill. There wasn't a pile of shit or used syringes to sidestep, so that was a win.

She walked past a series of dumpsters and parked cars, then skipped onto the sidewalk, heading east on Tenth Avenue toward Kings Soopers, the only grocery store within a five-mile radius.

Hannah stared down at the sidewalk, timing each step so as not to step on a crack—short steps, big steps, half steps, double steps. Avoiding the cracks at all costs.

Three blocks into the walk, a homeless man in a

wheelchair sat next to a bus stop, probably in his fifties and pushing three hundred pounds. He looked like he hadn't showered in weeks, and his left leg was amputated below the knee. The man was holding a weathered sign with a black sharpie: "Why Lie, I Need a Fucking Beer." Some sort of Labrador mix with numerous bald spots lay next to the right wheel.

Hannah stopped, and they made eye contact. She quickly looked at the dog and smiled.

"What's his name?" she asked.

"Him? That's Bandit," the man said, coughing.

Hannah crouched and extended her hand. Bandit sat up, and she started petting his head, massaging behind his ear. He began licking her forearm. She'd always preferred animals over people.

"Hi Bandit."

"Yeah, he's about all I got left. About the only one who's willing to put up with all my bullshit."

Hannah glanced up for a moment, then back down. She continued petting Bandit, and his tail incessantly slapped onto the sidewalk.

Standing, she pulled out her wallet and removed a five-dollar bill and three singles, handing the money to the man.

"I'm sorry, this is all the cash I have."

He reached a timid hand out and took the bills. "God bless. God bless you, my darling."

Hannah waved and then continued east on Tenth.

When she was done shopping, she placed the divider onto the conveyor belt and started taking items out of the basket. Four boxes of Pop-Tarts, two boxes of Cinnamon Toast Crunch, a gallon of milk, two Totino's pepperoni pizzas, four Snickers, a king-size bag of peanut M&M's, five cans of Friskies Salmon cat food, and five cans of Pedigree Gravy with Beef dog food. Her diet was like that of a fourteen-year-old boy whose parents were on vacation. Hannah's favorite meal was a bowl of cereal, and on most days, that was all she ate. But even with a high-sugar, high-carbohydrate diet, she'd never weighed more than a hundred pounds.

A couple with a baby was at the register in front of Hannah. They were close to her age, maybe a couple years older at the most. Hannah watched them. They smiled at her, and she smiled back. Hannah knew they loved each other, and loved being part of a family, and being parents, and probably owned a beautiful house in City Park or Congress Park, and the husband had a successful career, and the wife was a stay-at-home mom, and they went to dinner parties with their successful friends who also lived in their beautiful houses with their beautiful children. That was the life she'd never have.

As a teenager, Hannah had dreamt of a storybook wedding, a husband who was an architect, maybe an engineer, two kids, a boy and girl, the boy three years older to protect his younger sister, a house in the mountains with a garden in the backyard, and flowers, yes lots of flowers, Marigolds and Pansies and Salvias.

That dream had died a long time ago.

On her way home, she stopped at the homeless man and Bandit and handed him a grocery bag with the dog food, bananas, Snickers, and box of granola bars. He opened it up, looked into it, then looked back up at her, becoming teary-eyed.

"I don't know what to say," he said, wiping away a tear.

"Have a good night."

Hannah continued west on Tenth Avenue, popping M&M's into her mouth, avoiding the cracks at all fucking costs.

Near exhaustion, Tom rested his palm on the bark of a tree. It was jagged and somewhat sticky. The trees were endless—Douglas fir, ponderosa pine, Colorado blue spruce, and quaking aspen, some of them older than the first European settlers in America.

Growing up, he'd always loved being in the mountains. Hikes with his dad, ski vacations, weekend camping trips with the Boy Scouts, and one of the proudest moments of his life, a ten-day solo backpacking trip along the Colorado Trail covering almost a hundred miles.

Now he detested it up here.

The air was crisp and cold in his lungs with each breath. His knees hurt, his lips were numb, and his body was freezing from head to toe, but he continued up the mountain.

Sometime later it began to snow. The flakes flew large and heavy, limiting the visibility to thirty, maybe twenty feet. The wind momentarily stopped, and Tom could hear his heart pounding against his chest. He wiped away snot with the back of his hand.

Tom was somewhere around ten thousand feet, on the side of a mountain in Arapaho National Forest. The snow was unpacked, probably about two feet, and some spots closer to three. He could've jogged five miles in the time it took to barely cover one in this terrain.

He knelt and tightened the straps of his snowshoes. The last thing he wanted was a twisted ankle. An injury of that magnitude in this remote location, in sub-zero overnight temperatures, would near certainly mean a frozen grave.

As he stood up, a mountain bluebird landed about ten feet in front of him. Tom watched it. The bird looked up at him, then hopped toward Tom, and finally chirped twice before flying away. Tom was alone once more, in the vast forest, miles from the nearest human.

He started walking, and the snow cracked like a thin sheet of glass with every new step. He walked for a long time.

"That's not supposed to be up here," he muttered.

About twenty feet up the ridge, protruding out of the snow, were the handles of a plastic grocery bag. Tom hurried up the ridge but tripped on the snowshoes. Slowly, he stood and returned to the hurried pace.

Dropping to his knees, he pulled on the handle, but there was very little give. After digging a hole around the bag, he pulled again, this time succeeding. As he opened the bag and stared into it, he remained motionless for a long while, maybe a minute or more.

The bag contained nothing but trash, energy bar wrappers, ziplock baggies with a few crumbs, two empty Gatorade bottles, and two napkins.

"God damn it!"

Tom lay in the snow, eyes facing up at the dense white cloud formations, close to exhaustion. His throat was dry, and he coughed hard into his hands. He thought about how easy it'd be to sit down and never get back up.

After a couple minutes, he sat up and removed a map and a red Sharpie from his backpack. The map was torn and ragged and had notes, circles, lines, and crosses scattered over its surface. This was his eighteenth backcountry trip in the last month, and the bag of trash was the closest thing to a clue he had found. He was searching for a needle in a haystack that was over two thousand square miles, and the worst part was the needle might not even be there at all.

Standing, he side-stepped down the ridge, then looked back at his partially covered tracks. Pulling back his sleeve,

Tom revealed his Casio. It was 12:42. At least three hours of usable daylight, and four until the forest was completely dark. He turned north and continued up the mountain, stepping on fresh, undisturbed snow.

Lisa placed her hand on the metal handle and paused. She knew the store was open, but hesitated, knowing she was the first customer of the day. Staring at the faint reflection in the glass, she barely recognized the person she'd become.

Finally, she pulled the door open. A bell chimed, and a clerk popped up from behind the counter with a smile.

"Morning," he said.

Lisa gave a slight nod, then looked down, focusing on the tile while she navigated the store. She stopped at the second aisle and picked up a 750ml bottle of Smirnoff Vodka, wiping off the dust. Glancing back at the counter, she saw the clerk still smiling. Lisa returned a quick smile then turned away and grabbed two bottles of orange juice before walking back to the counter.

"Do you need anything else?" the clerk said.

"I'll take two packs of Marlboro Reds."

The bell rang and Lisa turned. An old man staggered into the store, then beelined straight toward the beer cooler without acknowledging her or the clerk.

She grabbed the brown paper bag and turned without saying a word. At the door, she glanced out of the corner of her eye and saw something she hadn't seen in a long time. Taped on the glass between the business hours and the Broncos' 1998 schedule was a flier.

MISSING PERSON
Megan Marie Floyd
Last seen December 12, 1996, Fraser, Colorado
Height: 5'4"
Weight: 117 pounds
Hair: Brown
Eyes: Green
Sex: Female
Race: White

It'd been months since she'd seen the poster, and it reminded her of a time when she still had hope that Megan would be found.

Lisa turned back to the clerk. "How long has this been hanging up?"

"What?"

"The Missing Person flier. How long has it been here?"

"Lady, I really have no idea. I started like a month ago, and I'm pretty sure it's been there the entire time."

"Well, I can tell you it's worthless at this point," Lisa said, ripping it off the window.

She crumpled up the flier and tossed it onto the ground. The clerk said something, but Lisa ignored him as she walked out and across the parking lot to her car. Placing the bag on the roof, she pulled out a bottle of orange juice, then dumped about half of it at her feet. She grabbed the bag, opened the door, and climbed into the car.

Staring out, she watched snowflakes fall onto the windshield and quickly evaporate into nothing. Snowflake then nothing, over and over and over again. She was mesmerized and watched this repeating cycle for some time.

Finally, she opened the bottle of Smirnoff and dumped it into the orange juice bottle until it was full again. She screwed on the lid, then gently shook the plastic bottle until the vodka and orange juice were properly mixed.

Lisa placed the bottle in the cup holder and rummaged through her purse, looking for an orange translucent prescription bottle. Locating the bottle, she opened it and dropped two white oval pills into her palm and instantly swallowed them, using the screwdriver as a chaser.

She hated the person she'd become. And the sad thing was, she knew there was nothing that could fix her.

After a few minutes, she started the car and pressed a cassette into the tape player. The opening bells of "Plainsong" by The Cure started to play. She listened until the chorus began, then pulled out of the parking spot and turned north onto Highway 40.

A gust of wind blew Hannah's hair into her eyes as she placed her hand on the headstone. The breeze rustled the last remaining leaves clinging to the branches above.

Gradually she bent down and kneeled in front of the headstone, then brushed away the dusting of snow and placed two white orchids at the base. After a moment of silence, she ran her hand across the inscription, staring without blinking.

Loving Daughter and Sister, Casey Rebecca Jacobs. June 15, 1969 - January 21, 1989.

"This never gets easier," Hannah said, wiping the tears off her hot cheek.

Growing up, Hannah had idolized Casey. She was the smart one, the funny one, the pretty one, the one their parents bragged about to their friends at parties.

"I was looking through pictures last week and found one from the night you borrowed Dad's car and were supposed to take me bowling, but you drove me up to that party in Laramie. I think that was the first time I ever smoked weed, and I remember I was so high and got so scared because I thought I was going to get in trouble for missing curfew, but you promised you'd get me home before midnight, and you did, with five minutes to spare." She paused for a second. "But if we would've left thirty minutes earlier like I said, you wouldn't have had to drive ninety down 287 while high to make it back in time."

Hannah smiled, but it quickly disappeared.

"That was like three months before you," she said, trailing off.

The look on Hannah's father's face when the police called was something no child should have to experience. That was the first time she'd ever seen him cry—up to that day, she thought he was invincible. He wasn't. Nobody was.

Hannah had been fifteen, and that was the first time she'd ever experienced loss. She'd never been to a funeral and never personally known someone who'd died. Hell, up to that point, the biggest tragedy in her life was watching the Challenger explosion.

Shortly after they buried Casey, the animosity between her parents grew, and the family began to disintegrate. Her dad drank to mask the pain, quickly becoming a full-blown alcoholic. Her mom became distant and detached, eventually moving out of the house and out of Fort Collins to Denver, never returning to the home the four of them had shared for more than a decade.

And for the first time in her life, Hannah was alone. She didn't have someone to suggest new bands to her, she didn't have someone to talk to about her latest crush, she didn't have someone to confide in, and she didn't have someone to make her laugh when she was sad. Her best friend was gone.

Three months after the funeral, Hannah decided to run away from home. She only had twenty dollars and no idea where to go, and after pondering her options, she decided to jump on the Fort Collins shuttle to Stapleton Airport.

She wanted to be anywhere but Colorado, and dreamt of getting on a plane and flying to Hawaii, or somewhere in Central America, or maybe even New Zealand. But even if she had the money for a ticket, and somehow was able to purchase it without parent consent, and somehow got past boarding, she knew she couldn't fly. She knew she couldn't even step foot on a plane without having a crippling panic attack.

The last time she'd flown was with Casey. Hannah was eleven, Casey fifteen, and they were flying back from Orlando after spending a week at their grandma's house. About an hour into the flight, the plane started to experience extreme turbulence. Then about a minute later, it started to plummet. It felt like it was dropping out of the sky.

There were a few seconds of eerie silence before the screams, and prayers being recited, and people vomiting. Probably every soul on that plane thought they'd be dead within minutes. Hannah was certain of it. Thoughts of never seeing her parents, or her friends, or her cat Felix consumed her, and she began to cry uncontrollably.

Then Casey grabbed Hannah's thigh and started to yell.

"Look at me. Look at me!"

Hannah turned, tears running down her face.

Casey squeezed tighter. "We're not going to die. I promise we're not going to die! Do you believe me?"

After a few moments, Hannah began nodding hysterically.

"Just close your eyes and think of good thoughts. This will be over soon."

Hannah leaned back and closed her eyes. Thoughts of the clear blue ocean water, and the waves crashing on her legs, and her feet in the sand. Then, as suddenly as it started, the plane leveled and began climbing. The captain's voice came over the intercom, but Hannah was so ecstatic it just sounded like gibberish.

"I told you everything would be okay," Casey said, wrapping her arms around Hannah.

That was the last time she'd flown, and she'd probably never fly again. Not without Casey. She was Hannah's Xanax, security blanket, and therapist all in one.

Katie stared into the trunk of her 1991 Toyota Corolla. Everything she owned was in there. It wasn't much: some clothes, about thirty CDs, a portable stereo and a shoebox full of pictures. The pictures were her most prized possession, and she'd do almost anything to protect them.

Just a couple loose ends to tie up, and she was gone. No plans to ever return to Colorado. She was a native, but Colorado had changed, and she knew it was time to leave. Time for a new beginning.

Her grandma owned a Victorian-style house, a small stable, and ten acres of land outside of Merriman, Nebraska, where she kept a chicken coop, plus three dogs and three horses. Riding the horses was Katie's first love, and she sorely missed it. The freedom they provided. Miles from anyone, just her and the animal.

She looked forward to small-town, country life. Fuck

the city, the skyscrapers and the people. She wasn't going to miss any of it.

Katie slammed the trunk and started across the Walmart parking lot.

Stopping about halfway down the aisle, Tom bent down and placed a fifty-pound bag of Purina dry dog food on the bottom shelf of his shopping cart. On his knees, he looked to the end of the aisle. A girl was standing there, half hidden behind an endcap, staring at him. They made eye contact for a few moments before she vanished.

Tom placed the groceries on the conveyor belt and leaned on the shopping cart. "The Christmas Song" by Nat King Cole played over the store intercom.

"My kids all live out of state, and my husband passed away two years ago, so I'm spending Christmas alone again," said an elderly woman at the register.

"I'm sorry to hear that," the cashier said.

"I'm used to it. It's part of growing old. Either you die, or you live long enough to become a burden to everyone around you. I just wish for one more Christmas with my grandchildren before I go."

The cashier nodded without looking up. He continued scanning items, but at a faster pace.

She turned back to Tom. "Merry Christmas."

"Merry Christmas to you as well," he said.

Old and alone, that was Tom's fate—well, if he survived to be a senior.

He placed the groceries into the 4Runner, then slammed the hatch and turned to return the shopping cart to the store.

"Mr. Floyd?" a female voice said from behind him.

Tom looked back. "Yes?" He studied the girl for a moment. "Do I know you?"

"No, we've never met, but I knew Megan through a mutual friend. And, umm, I just wanted to say I'm so sorry," she said. It looked like she was about to say something else, but the words just trailed off instead.

"Thank you," Tom said. "How did you guys know each other?"

The girl looked around the parking lot, watching as a minivan slowly drove toward them.

"I need to go," she said quietly.

Tom reached out and grabbed her forearm. She attempted to pull away, but he tightened his grip. He wasn't about to let her slip through his hands.

"How do you know Megan?" Tom said louder.

"I can't talk about it."

"Why not?"

"Because I know what will happen to me if I do."

Tom stared at the girl, trying to comprehend what she had just said. His heart pounding against his chest.

"Could you let go? It's really starting to hurt," she said, motioning to her arm.

Tom had tightened his grip without realizing it.

"What would happen to you if you talked to me?"

The girl searched the parking lot, then looked at him. "Can we go into your car?"

"If I let you go, are you going to run?"

"I promise I won't."

Tom released his grip and moved around the car to the driver's side. They walked in unison, and he watched her through the car windows like an eagle spying its prey. He got into the 4Runner, reached over, and opened the passenger door. The girl climbed in, then softly pulled the door closed, leaving it slightly ajar.

She pulled out a pack of Marlboro Reds. Tom had a lighter ready before she had the cigarette on her lips. She took a drag and gazed out the window at a patch of grass in a parking lot median, soon to be brown and dead.

"What's your name?"

"It doesn't matter. You have until I'm finished with this," she said, flicking the cigarette into the ashtray.

"How do you know Megan?"

"We met at this house up in Evergreen. There was a little party, maybe fifteen or twenty people. Drinking, smoking weed, doing some lines. You know, just a bunch of degenerate kids getting fucked up."

Tom had found some drug paraphernalia hidden in Megan's dresser. A couple pipes, a joint, and a baggie with coke residue. He chalked it up as teenage experimentation.

"Are you sure it was her?"

The girl nodded. "It was her."

"When was this party?"

"I don't remember the exact date, but it was definitely before she disappeared. I remember seeing her face on the news. I'd guess the first week of December."

"Who was she with?"

The girl shrugged.

"Whose party was it?"

She eyed the car door, pondering the question for a moment. Very slowly, she brought the cigarette to her lips and took a long drag.

Tom had arrested dozens of girls that looked like her. Druggies, runaways, sex workers. Twenty-somethings who lived too hard and would be lucky to see thirty. Girls who'd do almost anything to get their next fix—but this girl had a sincerity to her, something in her eyes that felt like she was trustworthy.

"There hasn't been a lead in the case for a long time,

so if you have any information about Megan, please tell me anything you know," Tom pleaded.

"I don't know his name, but from what I heard, he's a big-time dealer out of Evergreen. He supplies everyone up and down the 285 corridor. Meth, coke, acid, weed—you name it, he deals it."

"Take me to that house. Or give me directions, or draw me a map. Anything, please."

The girl chuckled. "Even if I wanted to, I couldn't. Those mountain roads are like a fucking maze. I could drive them for weeks and probably never find the place again."

"What about your friends—would they know where it was?"

The girl jammed the cigarette into the ashtray. "Your time is up."

Before Tom could react, she had both feet on the pavement. She glanced back and said, "I wish I could help. I really do."

"At least tell me your name," Tom said.

The girl smiled, then slammed the door and vanished behind a minivan. Tom jumped out and started the chase, hoping to get her car's make or model, or maybe even a license plate number, but she was gone, like a ghost in the night.

Standing at the office door, Hannah gently knocked three times then waited. A few moments later, she knocked again.

"Come in," Marshall muttered.

She walked into the office, then sat down across from him. He was flipping through the pages of a three-ring binder and didn't look up, seemingly unaware of Hannah's presence.

The office was cold—it was always cold, even in the dead of winter. Probably sub-seventy degrees. Hannah crossed her legs, zipped up her jacket, and started rubbing her hands together like she was standing over a campfire.

"Good morning," she finally said.

"Morning," Marshall said, hangover sweat seeping down his forehead.

"Long night?"

The room stank of nicotine and old whiskey barrels. The only thing Hannah loathed more than the smell of whiskey was the taste.

"What gave it away?"

"Hmm, you look like you haven't slept in days, you reek of cheap whiskey, and you're wearing the same clothes from three days ago. Want me to keep going?"

Marshall always had a rough look, like he'd stayed up until two in the morning drinking and smoking nonstop, but in the last few months, his appearance had rapidly deteriorated. His face was pale, ghostlike. It was contrasted by the dark, heavy bags under his bloodshot eyes.

Sometimes, she looked into those eyes and they were unrecognizable. Like she was across from a stranger. The drinking was bad, but it was the pills that worried her. He was playing Russian roulette with a bag of uppers and downers, and she knew it was a game he'd eventually lose.

"No, and thanks for always being honest," he said.

"Being honest is one of my few redeeming qualities."

Marshall picked up a coffee cup, drank the remaining sips, and placed it back on the table. Then he briefed Hannah on his meeting with Tom and Megan's disappearance.

"The dad is convinced it was Kevin Strand," Marshall said.

"It's pretty convenient to blame your missing daughter on the local serial killer."

"Yeah, and it's also been swaying him away from other possible suspects."

"So, there isn't any evidence that it could be him?"

"He lived two hours away and occasionally visited Fraser. Other than that, there's nothing."

"The grad student didn't have any connection to him either. She was just very unlucky. If she would've gotten to that trailhead two minutes later, he probably would've never seen her car, and she'd still be alive."

Marshall leaned back and did a couple arm stretches.

"I know, I've read the case file. It just doesn't fit his MO. Megan's car would've been found, her remains, her purse, something."

"I agree, but he shouldn't be removed as a suspect until we know for certain he wasn't involved."

"Duly noted," Marshall said. "We'll keep him as a suspect, but let's not spend a lot of time on him either. I'm more interested in the boyfriend, Jack." He started thumbing through the pages in the folder. "Jack Gardner. He lawyered up within days, didn't participate in a single organized search, and it sounds like he didn't give two fucks that she went missing."

"Maybe she thought their relationship was more than it was. Maybe he didn't care about her that much. Maybe he's a college kid three girlfriends removed."

"Maybe, but there's something that is off with the kid. They'd been friends since middle school, and were together for almost all of high school, so you'd think he'd display some compassion."

"It doesn't surprise me."

"And why is that?"

"I think you forget that twenty-year-old males are

complete assholes. All they care about is themselves and getting their dicks wet," Hannah said.

Marshall took out a cigarette and lit it. He removed an ashtray from the top drawer and placed it on the desktop. "I can see your wheels spinning—what are you thinking?" he asked.

"I'm still waiting to hear back from one of my guys, but I think I might have something," she said, opening a notebook.

Hannah had met Marshall shortly after her twentieth birthday. She'd answered a Help Wanted ad looking for an assistant. Basic office work: answering calls, filing, and some bookkeeping. She'd never worked in an office before and wasn't qualified, but as the only applicant, she was hired by default.

Four months into the job, Marshall got a DUI and lost his license. Driver was added to her duties, and shortly after that she started assisting on cases. Knocking on doors, minor surveillance, and background checks.

Two months later, she was promoted to Assistant Investigator and assigned to her own cases, starting with workman's comp, insurance fraud, and cheating husbands. Her biggest accomplishment to date was locating the daughter of a mother who was given up for adoption.

Marshall said she was a natural at being an investigator— he claimed it was her calling.

"What about Benjamin Paterson?" Hannah said.

"I haven't heard the name before," Marshall said, shaking his head.

"Well, he worked at the Fraser Market, in the deli, at the same time as Megan. He was questioned, cleared, and never talked to again. About a month after Megan went missing, he quits and moves to Las Vegas. He told everyone that he was moving home to take care of his sick mother."

"Go on."

"Well, his mother died in a car accident in 1990."

Marshall tapped on the desk. "Interesting."

"And in June, he broke into the apartment of a single twenty-one-year-old UNLV student who wasn't home. Luckily, a vigilant neighbor heard some unusual noises, looked outside, and saw someone climbing into a bedroom window and called 911. Police showed up, saw the screen window on the ground, and began a search of the apartment. Benjamin was found hiding in the bedroom closet. But since the girl wasn't home, and since he wasn't armed, they only charged him with second-degree burglary. He posted bail two days later and has never appeared at any of his subsequent court dates. Here's the kicker." Hannah paused. "Guess what their connection was?"

"They worked together?"

"Bingo. At a Target in Henderson. She was a cashier, and he worked in the warehouse. Those stores probably have a hundred, hundred fifty people working there, but I'd bet almost anything they'd at least seen each other in passing."

Marshall jammed the cigarette into the ashtray and immediately lit up another one, "So, this guy broke into an apartment of a girl he worked with, who could've been able to ID him."

"And she looks strikingly similar to Megan—same height, same body type, same hair color."

Hannah slid a picture of the girl across the desk.

"Jesus fucking Christ, if it wasn't for some nosy neighbor, there could be another missing girl who's an acquaintance to him."

Hannah nodded.

"And they just let that motherfucker walk out of jail?"

Marshall said, sucking on the cigarette.

She shrugged. "He posted bail."

"And please tell me you think he's in Denver," Marshall said.

Hannah nodded.

"When did you become so good?"

"I've always been this good. I think you're just finally paying attention."

Marshall smiled. "You keep working him, I'll work the boyfriend, and hopefully we'll get a lead out of one of these fuckers."

"Sounds good." Hannah got up and started toward the door.

"And page me if you get into a sticky situation or need some help. I'll come running."

"I know," she said without turning back.

Milo crossed Hannah's lap, pacing the edge of the bed like a tightrope walker as she stared at the number with a Las Vegas area code scratched onto a piece of paper. She was a little nervous about making the call, but if she were on the receiving end, she'd prefer it around 7 p.m. Not too late, not too early.

She twirled the cordless phone in her palm a few times, then pressed talk and began to dial. After the second ring, a girl answered.

"Hello?"

"Can I speak to Molly?"

"This is her."

"Hello Molly, my name is Hannah Jacobs, and I'm a private investigator from Denver. I was wondering if I could ask you some questions about Benjamin Paterson?"

"I'm sorry, I can't help you."

"Please, there's a girl from Colorado that went missing, and I think he might be linked to her." Hannah hurried the sentence. "All I ask for is five minutes."

There was a long silence before Molly spoke. "After he skipped his court date, I called the detective almost daily asking for updates. After a while, he stopped returning my messages. I figured they stopped looking for him. I honestly don't know if he will ever see jail time for what he did to me."

Hannah started to say something but quickly stopped. An ugly feeling coursed throughout her entire body.

Molly continued, "About a week after he broke in, I was doing laundry and noticed a stain on a pair of underwear. I took a closer look and realized it was semen. That fucking cocksucker jerked off onto my underwear." Her voice was faint. "I threw up right there, right in my fucking closet. I had to throw away every piece of clothing I owned."

Unsure of a response, Hannah mumbled, "I'm so sorry."

Without acknowledging her, Molly said, "I can't sleep, and every time I close my eyes I'm terrified that I'm going to wake up with him standing over me. I had to move, get a new job, drop out of school. He fucking ruined me."

"I understand if you don't want to talk, I really do, and I can't imagine how hard it is, but there's a girl who's been missing for over two years, and I think Ben might be involved."

"Why do you think he might have something to do with her?"

"They worked together, and he moved to Vegas about a month after she disappeared."

For a few moments, they each remained quiet, as if waiting for the other to speak.

"How can I help?" Molly finally said.

Hannah began asking questions. If she'd seen Benjamin—she hadn't. If she thought he was still in Las Vegas—she wasn't sure. If she knew anyone who was in contact with him—she didn't. If he ever mentioned friends or family in Denver—to her knowledge, he hadn't. Hannah asked a few more questions and all of the answers were "No" or "I'm not sure."

Hannah was about to end the call when Molly said, "Every so often I get a feeling that someone is following me, but it's probably just anxiety, and I don't know if it's me being freaking crazy or if it is actually someone."

"You're not crazy, I promise. It's completely normal to have those feelings after that kind of experience and to be anxious from time to time," Hannah said.

"I've been seeing a therapist, and she has helped me a little. I'm not a complete mess like I was, so I guess that's a good thing." Molly paused. "I just want that fucker to pay for what he did to me."

"So do I," Hannah said.

She thanked Molly and they said goodbye.

After hanging up, Hannah remained motionless for a minute or two, staring blankly at the phone. She felt guilty about making the call. She knew the girl probably wouldn't have any helpful information about Benjamin. All it did was unnecessarily open old scars.

Finally, she fell back onto the bed, slipped on her headphones, and pressed play on her Discman.

With her mind wandering, Lisa aimlessly watched the barista dump shots of espresso in various sizes of plastic cups and pump an assortment of flavors into them—French

Vanilla, Hazelnut, and Caramel. She momentarily turned to her sister sitting across the table, then turned back to the counter.

"Lisa, are you listening to me?" Claire said.

"Not really. What did you say?"

"I asked if you're still going to that grief counselor."

"No. No, I'm not."

"When did you stop going?"

"I think it was after the second or third visit."

"Jesus Lisa, how do you ever think you're going to get better?"

Lisa placed both hands flat on the table and leaned forward. "That's the thing—I'm not going to get better," she said with a blank face.

Being six years older, Lisa had never been close to her sister, and at times it was like they were from two different generations. Lisa was getting drunk while Claire was playing with dolls. Lisa left for college when Claire was entering middle school.

They never formed the bond that most sisters have, and they had come to terms with that, but after Megan disappeared, Claire had attempted to build the missing relationship. She wanted to be the shoulder to cry on, the older sister she herself had never had.

Lisa appreciated the gesture, but she preferred being alone with the heartache and heartbreak. The only reason she was at the coffee shop was that Claire had arrived at her house unannounced and forced her to go.

Claire took a sip of coffee. "What does Tom say about all this?"

"I don't know."

"Are you guys talking?"

"Not really. I honestly don't think we've been in the same room for more than five minutes since the summer.

He's off trying to be the hero and find Megan's killer." Lisa paused. "I don't know what's worse—him living in denial, but still holding on to hope and having a reason to wake up every day, or me, who's accepted the reality, but it's a hopeless one, and one I don't want to live in."

"Lisa, I'm really getting worried about you."

Lisa ignored Claire and stared out the window.

"I've been having these dreams about Megan. They are so fucking vivid, and it feels like we're really together, and for a brief moment each time I wake up, and still a little groggy I forget that she's gone. Those are the only times I've smiled in the last two years."

Tom white-knuckled the steering wheel as the Ford Taurus in front of him began to slide into the median. The car turned out of the slide at the last moment and fishtailed a few times until it was back between the highway lanes.

The windshield wipers and defrost were on high, but it was little help—visibility was thirty feet at best.

The highway was a disaster. Cars, trucks, and semis lay scattered along the shoulder, some having skidded in the snow and ice and some voluntarily pulled over, opting to wait out the storm or wait for a rescue, whatever came first.

In his early twenties, he'd driven over Vail Pass in complete whiteout conditions near midnight. He couldn't see the road, or any signs, or the guardrail, or any vehicle tracks, or if he was even driving on the highway or about to drive off it. The snow was coming down so hard that turning off the headlights actually improved visibility. That was his worst winter drive; this was a close second.

Tom looked down at the speedometer—twenty-six. Even at this speed, the drive felt extremely dangerous, and he was somewhat surprised CDOT hadn't closed I-25 south of Castle Rock. Monument Hill could be treacherous in light dustings, but this was a full-on winter blizzard that even native Coloradoans wouldn't scoff at.

The sun began to set as Marshall twisted a cigarette into the car ashtray next to almost a dozen butts. As he rolled down the window, smoke billowed out of the car. He turned the key, switched the heat to the highest setting, and began rubbing his hands in front of the vent.

The car was parked in front of a single-story duplex ten blocks from the CU campus in Boulder. For almost an hour, nobody had come or left the duplex, and he hadn't seen any activity inside.

Marshall stepped out of the car and walked to the mailbox. He opened it and started flipping through the mail. It was mostly junk mail, grocery store ads, and catalogs addressed to the "Current Resident," but there was an electricity bill addressed to Jack Gardner. He put everything back into the mailbox and closed it.

Casually, he walked across the grass, then onto the brick pathway that led to the front door. Peeking in the window, he saw a shadow walk across a hallway into what was presumably a kitchen. Marshall pressed the doorbell and heard the chime through the door. On his fingers, he counted to five Mississippi, then pressed the doorbell again. He started the count once more, but stopped on three when he heard footsteps walking toward the door.

The door opened a couple inches.

"I'm looking for Jack Gardner," Marshall said.

After a brief pause, it opened a few more inches.

"I'm Jack. What can I help you with?" A head appeared from behind the door.

Marshall recognized the face from the file, but the man looked much younger. Jack was twenty-three but could've easily been mistaken for a teenager with his babyface.

"I was wondering if I could ask you some questions about Megan Floyd."

"If you have any questions, you can talk to my lawyer."

"It should only take a few minutes."

"Fuck off!" Jack shouted.

The kid started to shut the door, but Marshall stuck his boot into the opening, stopping it.

"Get the fuck off my property before I call the damn cops."

"Good luck with that, kid. I know the average response time of Boulder PD, and it's about nine minutes, probably longer for a male caller who doesn't have a bullet in him. I guarantee I'll be long gone before anyone shows up."

That was a lie, but Marshall had a hunch Jack was gullible enough to buy it. There was a short pause.

"So, you're not a cop?"

"I am not a cop," Marshall said, shaking his head slowly.

"If you aren't a cop, why the fuck would I talk to you about Megan?"

"Because I don't have to follow the Department Operations manual or the Code of Ethics or any fucking guidelines a cop has to adhere to. And that means I can make up my own rules, and I'll continue to bother you until you answer my questions. So what do you say, Jackie Boy? Answer my questions now, and you'll never see my face again."

"You have two minutes," Jack said begrudgingly.

"When was the last time you talked to Megan?" Marshall asked.

"Like I've stated countless times before, she called me in the middle of the night like a month before she went missing."

Marshall remembered that from Megan's landline call records. It was a twenty-seven-minute call at 3:29 a.m. on November 12. Exactly one month before she disappeared.

"What did you guys talk about?"

"It was mostly her. She was apologizing for being a bad girlfriend and said I deserved better. She was rambling, not making much sense."

"Sounds like she was on something," Marshall said.

"You think?"

"Do you know what she was using?"

"I caught her doing blow a handful of times and we fought about it. Don't get me wrong, I like to party as much as anyone, but I don't fuck around with powder. That shit will rot your fucking brain."

"Is that why you broke up?"

"That's part of it. And I just felt the relationship had kinda run its course. I was at school, and she was up in Granby, and I didn't really want to be tied down in a relationship."

"You mean you wanted to fuck other girls," Marshall said.

"That's one way to put it."

"How'd the call end?"

"She told me she loved me and asked if we could grab lunch sometime. I said sure, I'd give her a call when I got to my parents for Thanksgiving break."

"Did you?"

"Nah, I forgot."

"I didn't see your name on any of the search party

signup lists. Did you forget about those too?" Marshall said.

"Dude, I had too much going on at the time. Finals, my Mexico vacation. Just life shit."

Marshall studied Jack for a long moment without speaking. He hated to admit it, but Hannah was right. This kid was an asshole, and he probably wasn't responsible for Megan's disappearance.

He thanked the kid and started back across the lawn.

THREE

B uilt-in 1871, Colorado State Penitentiary was Colorado's oldest prison, predating statehood. The nondescript, brick building sat at the edge of the Great Plains high desert, with the Sangre de Cristo Mountain Range, home to some of the state's highest mountain peaks, forty miles to the west.

Outside the building lay a series of twelve-foot-tall fences wrapped in barbwire, with watchtowers at each corner manned by correctional officers carrying high-power rifles. The penitentiary was home to almost a thousand inmates, including four on death row—one being Kevin Strand.

Tom leaned back against the 4Runner with one foot against the door panel and guided a trembling cigarette into his mouth. He inhaled, going over the questions in his head like a quarterback preparing for the big game.

Tom had requested this meeting over a year ago, but was constantly bumped for news magazine shows like *Dateline* and *48 Hours* as well as journalists and seventeen meetings with the author who penned the recently published New York Times bestseller true crime book simply titled, *A Killer in the Mountains.*

Finally, with the assistance of the Grand County sheriff and the state senator from Colorado's 8th district, Tom was granted a two-hour meeting with Kevin under the pretense that he was investigating unsolved missing person cases in Colorado and southern Wyoming.

Two hours to sit face-to-face with the man who could've killed Megan. *Don't show your nerves, don't let him take control, don't let that fucker get in your head. And most importantly, don't let him know you are Megan's father.*

Tom glanced down at his watch, then lit another cigarette.

"Ten minutes. Ten more minutes," he whispered.

The final notes of "Mother's Little Helper" by The Rolling Stones rang out as the door closed behind Hannah, taking the sunlight with it. She stood in the bar entrance, waiting for her eyesight to adjust to the darkness. There were few customers, mostly derelicts, along with the bartender and Doug. They acknowledged each other with a nod, and she started toward him.

"Could you have picked a seedier place to meet?"

"Only the best for you, my darling," Doug said.

They hugged, and Hannah sat at the bar next to him. She looked up at the old Panasonic TV hanging above the bar, the volume muted on an infomercial for a home gym. The smells of stale beer, vomit, and thirty years of cigarette smoke were entwined in the stained carpet. The bartender shuffled over, and she ordered a screwdriver.

"Vodka before noon?" Doug asked.

"And orange juice. Orange juice is key. I'm getting Vitamin C as well as a little booze," she said with a smile.

"Hey, I'm not judging. Just making an observation."

"How the hell have you been? Staying out of trouble I hope?" Hannah said.

"Never been better, and no, me and trouble go hand in hand."

An older drunk stumbled up to Hannah and tapped her shoulder. She did a quarter turn and gave him a quick once-over.

"Why don't you ditch this loser and come spend a night with a real man," the drunk said.

She smiled and batted her eyes.

"Sir, even if you could get it up, which I'm guessing hasn't been the case in at least a decade, I'm positive that you'd probably have a heart attack if you saw me naked. And I really don't want to explain to the paramedics why some prick dropped dead. Now, go back to your stool, and please leave us alone."

The drunk stared at her, plainly trying to think of a response, but with none rising in his addled head, he slowly turned and walked away.

"Sorry about that," Hannah said turning back to Doug. "What do you got for me?"

"I found Ben," Doug said.

"You fucking found him already? It's only been three days."

The bartender dropped off the screwdriver, and Hannah grabbed the sliced orange off the rim. She took a bite, then dropped the peel back into the glass and took a drink.

"Shit, Denver is a fucking cow town—everybody knows everybody, and if you have the right currency, it's not that hard to find someone," Doug said.

"Where is he?"

"At The Rusty Nickel off Colfax and Federal. One of my clients is a bartender there and said Ben's been going in almost every night for the last two weeks.

"Are you sure it's him?"

Doug nodded. "I went there last night, and sure as shit it's him. He was getting drunk by himself and playing songs from the jukebox. After last call, he stumbled down Colfax to the Lakewood Motel and into room number seven."

"I fucking love you," Hannah said.

Doug smiled, looking somewhat embarrassed.

"And for the twentieth time, if you ever wanna come work for us, we'll hire you in a second," Hannah said.

"Thanks for the offer, but doing what I do pays better and is a lot more exciting."

Marshall spent the better part of a day poring over hundreds of pages of official case files, hoping there was something in there that everyone had overlooked or missed, something that would provide a clue as to what happened to Megan, but there wasn't. She'd vanished without a trace.

In a notebook, Marshall jotted down four possible theories.

Theory one: she upped and ran away. Possible, but unlikely. She would've only had the clothes on her back, the items in her car, and the money in her pocket. She had $1,500 in checking and almost $2,500 in savings. That money had never been touched, and her ATM card had never been used. The last time she made an ATM withdrawal was a week before she disappeared, for $60. If she'd decided to start a new life, it would've been virtually penniless.

Theory two: her car slid off the highway and down a ditch out of view. Highly unlikely. This did occur—just the year before, a woman driving back from lunch on 285 slid off the highway and down a hundred-foot embankment. She was found six days later with both legs broken, severely dehydrated and on the verge of death. But the search for Megan was one of the biggest Missing Person Searches in Colorado history, and almost every highway in Grand County had been searched multiple times by multiple people. If somehow that search missed the car, once the snow started to melt, someone would've seen it from a highway or trail. The vehicle would've been found.

Theory three: she was abducted and murdered by a complete stranger. Possible, but very unlikely. Despite high-profile news stories, stranger homicide was extremely rare, especially in Grand County. Kevin Strand was living in the county at the time, but he was virtually cleared of Megan's disappearance, and the odds of having two murderers living simultaneously in the same vicinity and killing in a sparsely populated county would be astronomical. Megan would've had better odds of being struck by lightning.

Theory four: she was abducted and murdered by someone she knew. In Marshall's opinion, this was the most likely scenario. Maybe it was the guy at the coffee shop who Megan was friendly with, or maybe it was a coworker or old classmate who was infatuated to the point that it became deadly. But how did they do it without leaving a single piece of evidence, and where was her car?

Sometime later, Marshall opened the copy of Megan's journal and started turning the pages. The first few were mostly doodles—mountains, landscapes, and animals. Nothing particularly good. About a third of the way through, there were word-for-word copies of poems: E. E. Cummings, "I Carry Your Heart"; Walt Whitman,

"Whispers of Heavenly Death"; and Robert Frost, "Stopping by Woods on a Snowy Evening," among others. Marshall read each poem a few times before turning the page.

Toward the back, there was a list of bands, venues, and dates: Radiohead/Ogden/10-5-95, Oasis/Mammoth/12-15-95, Sublime/Ogden/2-27-96, Warped Tour/Red Rocks/7-14-96, Primus/Red Rocks/7-19-96, Smashing Pumpkins/McNichols/8-30-96, Beck/Ogden/10-4-96, Fugazi/Mammoth/10-12-96, Tool/Mammoth/11-5-96, Mazzy Star/Ogden/11-11-96. The last entry was Weezer/Ogden/12-13-96. It was circled and underlined.

On the second-to-last page, toward the bottom, was a phone number with the name "Jenny" underneath it. Marshall picked up the phone and dialed. Disconnected. Marshall scribbled down different combinations of the last four digits—reversed order, last number first, first number last. When he was finished, there were twenty-four different combinations on the paper. He picked up the phone and started dialing. Numbers one through five were disconnected, but the sixth combination rang.

"Can I talk to Jenny?" Marshall said.

"Jennifer? I haven't seen her since she got arrested," an older woman said, sounding somewhat frail and drunk.

"Would you happen to know if she's still in jail?"

"No, she called up here like two weeks ago asking for money, and I told her if she wants some money, she should get a job like everyone else. Then she tells me she's working at Denny's, and I say why the hell are you calling me and begging for money if you got a job? Then she said a few words I'd rather not repeat and hung up."

"Did she mention what Denny's she was working at?" Marshall said.

'The one up in Lakewood."

"Off Union and Sixth?"

"Yeah, that's the one." The old lady paused. "Who is this, anyway?"

"An old friend. Thank you for your time, ma'am."

Marshall hung up and tapped the paper with the tip of the pen.

The interview room was cold. The wooden tabletop was cold, the tile looked cold, the bricks looked cold, and he knew the bars on the outside of the window were freezing. Tom shifted the chair, and it produced a loud squeak that echoed throughout the room. He looked down at his watch, then wiped the sweat from his upper lip. Over the course of his career, he'd questioned numerous killers, but to his knowledge, he'd never talked one-on-one with a serial killer.

The door finally opened, and Kevin walked into the room with a prison guard closely following.

Standing at five foot seven and 155 pounds soaking wet, with wireframe glasses and a receding hairline, he looked more like a computer repairman than one of the most sadistic killers of the twentieth century. His eyes were kind, and welcoming, but those eyes were some of the last images that at least six women saw. Kevin stopped at the table, cracked his neck, then sat across from Tom and smiled.

"Would you like me to stay?" the guard said.

"No, I'm good. Thank you," Tom said.

"Okay. You've got two hours. Press this button if you need anything," the guard said, pointing to an intercom next to the door.

Tom thanked him, then opened his folder and looked at Kevin.

"Hello Kevin, I'm Tom Floyd, and I was wondering if I could ask you some questions."

Kevin's eyes roamed the room, seemingly unimpressed by Tom and the lack of camera equipment. Then he turned to the window and stared for a few moments. "I hear there's a pretty bad storm out there."

"Yeah, six to ten inches in the Front Range and over three feet in the mountains—25 and 70 are closed in almost every direction. All the flights out of DIA have been canceled. They say it's the worst storm since the blizzard of '82."

"That was the Christmas Eve one, right? I was stuck in my house for five fucking days with my family. We were worried the roof was going to cave in," Kevin said, still staring out the window.

"Yeah, that one dumped a little over two feet in twenty-four hours. Pretty much incapacitated Denver for almost a week."

Kevin nodded for a few moments. "I really miss the snow. Being in the courtyard for an hour a day just doesn't cut it for me. It just feels different behind these walls, you know, almost like a manufactured snow. Fuck, I'd give anything to see one last snowfall up in Rocky Mountain National Park."

"There is something magical about the snow up there," Tom said.

"Ever been to Emerald Lake?"

"Yeah, a handful of times."

"In the winter?"

"Snowshoed that entire area about five years ago."

"Lucky bastard. It's like a Bob Ross painting up there—the frozen lakes, the towering mountain peaks and snow-covered trees. I wanna say, in the winter it's my favorite place in the entire country, and I've been to thirty-three states and fourteen National Parks, so I have a pretty decent sample size. I do regret never making it to Alaska, though. I hear amazing things, but I think we both know I'm not going to make that trip."

In an alternate universe, Tom could see being friends with Kevin, and that gave him an uneasy feeling.

"It's on my to-do list," Tom said.

Kevin cut him off. "I've been thinking a lot about my, um, final day. It's coming up pretty quick, less than two hundred days. At first, I just wanted it to come, but as it gets closer, I'm becoming hesitant and a little nervous. Knowing the exact day and time you're going to die really fucks with your head."

Kevin turned to the window, then took a long drink of water.

"But in an odd way, I'm kinda lucky. I get to plan what my final thoughts will be, and that's a privilege a lot of people don't get. Some schmuck that gets T-boned by an eighteen-wheeler doesn't have that opportunity. I, on the other hand, know the exact minute I'm going to die, and I consider that a luxury. I think my final memory is going to be of Emerald Lake, sitting on a few feet of ice, watching the snow come down and bluebirds circling above me."

Tom leaned back and studied the man, while Kevin looked at the pack of Camel Lights on the table.

"Can I get one of those?" Kevin said.

Tom removed two cigarettes, then pushed them across the table.

Leaning over the Denny's hostess station, Marshall studied the map of the restaurant. Red dry-eraser markings divided it into three sections, one for each server—Kim, Greg, and Jennifer. Jennifer's section was about six tables in the rear of the restaurant. Marshall leaned back as the hostess approached.

"Just you this afternoon?"

Marshall nodded. "Could I get a booth over there?" he said, pointing to Jennifer's station.

"Of course," she said.

He sat down and searched the menu while simultaneously tapping on the table with his thumb in a two, two, one pattern. A few minutes later, Jennifer lumbered out of the kitchen and over to Marshall's table. They briefly exchanged smiles. Marshall glanced down to the name tag pinned onto her collared shirt, which just read "Jen."

"What are you having to drink today?" she asked, avoiding eye contact.

"I'll take a coffee with some Sweet'n Low."

Jennifer smiled and nodded. "You got it. I'll be right back."

Six minutes later she returned with the coffee, but no packets of artificial sweetener. Marshall thanked her, then ordered a Denver omelet and hash browns with an English muffin.

He sipped on the coffee and watched Jennifer walk between the kitchen and various tables, barely acknowledging the customers.

About ten minutes later, Jennifer dropped off the food, then walked back into the kitchen. Tom ate, paid the bill, and returned to his car in the parking lot. He lit a cigarette and leaned into the steering wheel, watching the restaurant.

Sometime later, Jennifer walked out of the restaurant and started across the parking lot. Marshall quickly followed.

"Jennifer?" he said.

His voice startled the girl, and she sharply turned back. She studied him for a few moments, then started rummaging through her purse, probably searching for a knife or a can of pepper spray. Marshall took one step back, attempting to look less threatening.

"Do I know you?" she said.

"No. My name is Marshall York, and I was wondering if I could ask you some questions about a case I'm working."

"Let me see your badge."

"I'm a private investigator, and it's illegal for a PI to carry a badge in Colorado. They don't want us to be confused with the police. The best I can do is a business card."

"If you're not a cop, go fuck off!" Jennifer said, extending a middle finger.

She turned, but before she could take a step, Marshall had clutched her bicep. He squeezed his fingers and leaned into her ear.

"I'll let you decide, Jennifer—either you have a quick conversation with me right now, or I call your PO and tell him you're connected to an unsolved missing person case and we all go down to the station and have a nice, long conversation," Marshall whispered.

"You're fucking lying!"

"Then explain to me why your name and number was in Megan Floyd's journal."

She froze for a moment, then seemed to give up the struggle. "There's a picnic table back there," she said, gesturing behind the Denny's.

After they sat down, she fixated her eyes on the rivets

in the table, running her index finger across the wood like she was drawing a picture.

Marshall felt sorry for the girl. She looked defeated, like life had gotten the better of her and taken her down the wrong path, one she'd never anticipated.

"How did you find me?" she said.

"I decoded the number. Teenage girls have used that method for years when hiding a phone number."

"Fuck. After the first few months passed, I thought for sure nobody would come asking about her," she said, shaking her head aggressively.

"Why was your name in her journal?"

"Mr. York, I've done some things that I'm not proud of, but I got clean. Almost six months, and I go to a meeting three times a week. It's been really helpful, and I met a guy there. He's sober too, so that's kinda nice."

"Congratulations, that's great." He paused for a moment. "Jennifer, I'm trying to solve Megan's case, nothing more, and I could really use your help, so please, answer my questions and you can be on your way."

Jennifer exhaled, followed by a subtle cough.

"She was my dealer. It started out as small bags once, maybe twice a week, but quickly got out of hand. The time-tested story of the recreational user transformed into a junkie. I'd buy from her and turn around and sell to friends, neighbors, coworkers, pretty much anyone who wanted small quantities. By the end, I was buying a couple ounces every few days."

This surprised Marshall. Tom had implied Megan was an occasional user, but her being a dealer completely changed the circumstances of the case. This supported his theory that she was abducted by someone she knew. She could've been murdered during a drug deal gone wrong. That was something that happened every day in America.

Marshall leaned in. "Meth?"

The girl looked at him with wondering eyes, then nodded.

"Were you buying from her up until she disappeared?"

She nodded again. "The last time I saw her was like a week before she went missing."

"Do you know who was supplying her?"

"His name is Nathan. Rumors have it he's one of the biggest dealers in town."

Adrenaline rushed through Marshall's body. He had the first substantial lead, the name of a suspect.

"Did you ever meet him?"

"Once. Well, if you consider sitting in the car, nodding hello, then avoiding eye contact as meeting, then yes. White guy, brown hair, decent looking, probably late twenties, but guessing a meth addict's age adds a layer of complexity."

"Anyone else you know who's met Nathan?"

"Yeah, my friend Bryan. I think they actually hung out a few times."

"Could you introduce me to him?"

She shook her head. "He's dead. Drove into the back of a semi doing ninety down on C-470 last July."

"I'm sorry," Marshall said.

The girl smiled, then looked down at her watch and quickly stood up. "I have to get going or I'm going to miss my bus. Good luck with your investigation. I truly hope you find her."

"What do you think happened?" Marshall said.

"I don't know."

"No theories? No guesses? Nothing?"

Jennifer shook her head. "I try not to think about it."

Marshall watched the girl walk across the parking lot until she disappeared behind the building. After a few moments, he removed his notepad, flipped to an empty page, and wrote the name "Nathan," underlining it three times.

Anxiously Tom glanced at his watch. It'd been thirty-eight minutes, and Kevin had dominated the conversation, talking about places he missed, foods he missed, thoughts on the stock market, the Broncos, and his lawyer. He despised his lawyer and wished he could have ten minutes alone with him. The incoherent ramblings of a paranoid schizophrenic with borderline personality disorders.

Ten minutes into the conversation, Tom had slid a binder containing pictures of missing women, including Megan, across the table, and on three different occasions Kevin started to open the binder but slammed it shut before looking at the first picture. It was like he was toying with Tom.

Kevin leaned in, turned to the window, then slowly cracked his knuckles on each hand.

"I grew up in this tiny house outside of Nederland that was built in the twenties. My grandpa built it with some drinking buddies and lived there until the day he died. My grandma didn't last much longer after he passed, and we moved in before the dirt settled on her grave. It was more like a shack than a house—two bedrooms, one bathroom, and a tiny room in the back that I shared with my sister. There were seven of us living in something that was a little over five hundred feet. Do you want to know the worst part?"

"Do tell," Tom said.

"After I moved out, we learned that everything in the house was lead based. The paint, the pipes, the faucets, everything. Every ounce of water I drank and bathed in from eight to eighteen contained toxic levels of lead."

"And you think the lead is what made you kill all those girls?"

"The lead was the source, Mr. Floyd. It started me down a precise path. Have you ever heard of intrusive thoughts?"

"Like unwanted thoughts? Doesn't almost everyone have them from time to time?"

"Yes, but not everyone obsesses over them. And they don't become uncontrollable with everyone. And not everyone acts out on them."

"And not everyone who has them turns into a killer."

"True. I was very good at controlling them in my teens, but by my early twenties I was fighting the urge of wanting to drive directly into oncoming traffic, or jump off my fourth-story balcony, or abduct the pretty girl who worked at the library and cut her into little pieces. And right now, I'm fighting the urge to jump over this table, grab that pen, and start stabbing it into your eye sockets until you stop breathing," Kevin said with a faint smile.

Tom stared the monster in the eyes, not wanting to show any sign of weakness. He had six inches and almost fifty pounds on Kevin, and under normal circumstances he wouldn't think twice, but a psychopath was two feet across from him. It'd probably take thirty seconds, maybe a minute, for the guards to get in the room and restrain Kevin if he tried anything, and Tom was 90 percent sure he'd be able to defend himself during that time. It was the 10 percent that really worried him.

Tom casually scratched his chin. "I'd rather you didn't."

"I won't. You seem like a good guy, and I'm able to control them today, but sometimes they do get the better of me."

"Thanks, I appreciate that."

Kevin lit a cigarette. "Two weeks ago I was in my cell, and I dropped my pen and it fell under the bunk. I start reaching for it, but nothing, so I crawl under my bed, flick a lighter, and start searching for it. While I was down there, I saw something etched into the brick. It said *JGG was here. 1-1-57.* I start doing some investigation work, and it turns out I was in the same cell as Jack Gilbert Graham. Do you know who he is?" Kevin said.

"I don't," Tom said, shaking his head.

"Well, Jack has the distinction of being Colorado's first mass murderer. He put a time bomb composed of twenty-five sticks of dynamite inside a Christmas present and placed that present inside his mother's suitcase, then drove her to Stapleton Airport. He checked her luggage, said goodbye to her, then purchased an insurance policy from a vending machine and watched from the terminal as the plane took off."

He paused and took a drag.

"Two balls of fire fell from the sky and crashed into a field ten miles outside of Longmont. That crazy fucker killed forty-four people without even blinking an eye."

"I'm sorry, but I don't understand why you're telling me this."

"Because not all killers are the same."

Tom cleared his throat. "You raped and tortured a fifteen-year-old girl over the course of three days, before strangling her, dismembering her, and disposing of the body throughout Arapaho National Forest."

"I regret that one. She was nice, really nice. Even up to the end she was—she told me I could do whatever I wanted to her. She just wanted to live. I should've let her go," Kevin said, turning toward the window.

"And you don't see the correlation between you and Jack?"

"I don't understand killing innocent people for revenge, or jealousy, or money."

"But it's fine to kill someone for your own sick, twisted pleasure?" Tom said, almost yelling.

"I couldn't control my urges. I tried therapy, and medication, and meditation, and lived an isolated life, but the urge was too strong to fight. He dropped a plane from five thousand feet into a beet field, killing forty-four innocent people for money. His sole motivation was collecting on the insurance policy worth $37,500. That comes out to $852 a life." Kevin paused. "I had to do what I did and acted on my instincts, and if you can't see the difference between those, I really can't help you."

"And you think since you can't control your thoughts, you should be treated differently?"

"No, not at all, and that's why me and good 'ol Jack have one common bond." Kevin jammed a cigarette into the ashtray. "He was executed in the gas chamber a few hundred feet from this room, and in about six months, I'll have a lethal injection cocktail running through my veins."

When "Only in Dreams" by Weezer finished, Hannah turned off the car and stepped into the slush on Colfax Avenue. Reaching into her pocket, she pulled out three quarters and slid them into the parking meter.

She walked west on the sidewalk past a For Lease sign in a storefront window, then three guys wearing Guardian Angels jackets and red berets, then an alley where a man was urinating on a dumpster. Stopping at a crosswalk, she glanced across the street to a small, open grassy space with about a dozen tents and shopping carts and countless piles of trash. This twenty-block stretch of Colfax was a cesspool of dealers, addicts, prostitutes, and criminals. Hannah was certain that if Ben was still in Denver, this was where he'd be.

She crossed the street and walked into a 7-Eleven, where she purchased a pack of Marlboro Lights and a red lighter. Always red, always. She walked out of the store, tore open the pack of smokes, dropped the cellophane into the trash, lit a cigarette, then saw the purple-and-yellow neon sign of the Lakewood Motel.

A bell rang as Hannah walked into the lobby of the motel. In the window was a neon "Open" sign producing a constant buzz and a sign on the window sill with "NO TRESPASSING, NO PROSTITUTION, NO DRUGS – YOU WILL BE PROSECUTED" in a bright red font. An old man appeared from behind the curtain.

"How effective is that sign?" Hannah said.

"What do you think?"

"I'm guessing about as good as keeping the bedbugs out of the sheets."

"You'd be correct. What can I do for you darling?"

She placed a four-by-six picture of Ben on the counter. "Have you seen this man?"

"I'm sorry, I can't divulge that type of information."

She placed a twenty on the counter.

"Ma'am, like I said, I can't divulge that."

"I just have some simple questions. You can nod yes or no if you want."

She placed another twenty on the counter. The old man inspected Hannah from top to bottom.

"If I was twenty years younger, I'd ask you to my room and tell you anything you wanted to know."

"If you were twenty years younger, and I was twenty years older, I'd take you up on that offer," Hannah said with a smile. The old man began to turn red. She pushed the bills toward him. "C'mon, how about you help a pretty girl out."

"Yeah, he's staying here. He's been here about two weeks," he said in a soft drawl.

"Did you get a copy of his ID?"

"ID? This isn't a Hilton, sweetheart."

"Do you have a name?"

"Let me see." The old man reached under the counter and retrieved a hotel logbook. He started flipping through the pages. "Let's see, I think he started staying here in early December." The man stopped. "Here it is. Charles Reid, room seven."

"And Charles is this guy here?" she said, pointing at the picture.

"Yeah, I'm positive. He came in here the other day complaining about no hot water and I told him he was lucky he had any running water."

Hannah thanked the clerk, then walked out of the motel. She slid headphones over her ears and continued west on Colfax, avoiding the cracks at all costs.

It'd been ninety-five minutes. Tom was moments from throwing in the towel when Kevin turned his attention to the binder. He stared at it intently for a long, silent moment, then opened the cover and stared at the first picture.

All of the girls except Megan had gone missing after Kevin was arrested and were last seen in the Northeast. This was a safety measure to ensure Kevin didn't know any of the girls and to see if he'd lie about any abductions he couldn't have been responsible for.

Tom spent the entire morning contemplating where

he should place Megan's picture. Finally, he decided he'd flip a coin to make the decision. Heads, the fourth position, tails, the fifth. The coin landed on tails.

Kevin meticulously studied each picture, spending a minute or two on each one before licking his fingers and turning the page. On the fourth picture, he began tapping his index finger on the nose of a blond female in her early twenties.

"Her lips remind me of Amy," Kevin said. He stopped tapping on the picture and looked up at Tom. "Where did this girl go missing from?"

"I'm not giving you any information about these girls. I'm only here to see if you're connected with their disappearance, nothing more," Tom said.

"Amy was a fighter, she really was," Kevin said as he slid his finger across the picture. "As I was about to grab her, she turned and punched me in the face and ran. She was petite, but she could throw a punch. It fucking stung, and it took me a few seconds to catch my breath. The funny thing is, if she would have run toward the highway, she would've been saved, because a work truck drove past about twenty seconds later, but she ran into the forest, where the only person that could've saved her was me."

Kevin leaned in and lowered his voice.

"She fucking fought me all the way to the car, and if it wasn't for putting up such a fight, I still might be out there doing very, very bad things."

"Everyone in Colorado is grateful that she was such a fighter."

"Yes, she saved a lot of people misery."

Kevin smiled, then reached to turn the page to the fifth picture, Megan's picture. The room became eerily quiet as Tom watched him turn the page. It felt like everything was moving in slow-motion. His arms became heavy, like gravity was pushing down on him.

Kevin studied the picture, and Tom studied Kevin. Both of them remained motionless; the only sound was their muted exhales, almost synced. After a minute, Kevin looked up.

"I know this girl," he said.

"How?" Tom asked, leaning in.

"In passing, I guess you can say."

"From where?" Tom said, becoming rigid.

"She worked at that grocery store in Fraser. Umm, the Fraser Market or something. One time I was a little short on a pack of smokes, and she told me not to worry about it. I really appreciated that. She had a very luscious smile. I never forget a smile like that."

Tom jumped out of the chair, sliding it back across the floor. "You said had—she *had* a very luscious smile."

"Yes, I did. I remember reading about her in the papers. Megan, isn't it? She left work and was never seen or heard from again; one of the largest search-and-rescue efforts in the history of Grand County resulted in nothing, zero. Very unfortunate, very unlucky." Kevin began moving his fingers over the picture, almost like he was playing with her hair.

Tom reached across the table and yanked the folder away from Kevin, slamming it shut in one swift motion. He wanted to jump over the table and wrap his hands around the man's neck. Two years of pent-up rage was boiling over.

"Did you take her?" Tom shouted.

Kevin stared lifelessly for a brief moment, then shook his head. "No, I didn't."

"You're fucking lying! Where is she? Where is she!" Tom yelled at the top of his lungs.

"If I hurt this girl, I'd come clean, because in six months,

I'm going to be walking down death row, and when I'm strapped to that table I wanna have a clear conscience. You get my drift? I've told you all I know about Megan, and I wish you luck finding her, but if you're here, talking to me, her fate is already sealed."

"Rot in hell you piece of shit."

The interview had been a Hail Mary—deep down, Tom knew Kevin hadn't abducted Megan. There was no evidence, nothing linking him to her. All of the cars of his victims had been found. Megan's was still missing. He kept a memento of every victim, usually a necklace or ring. None of Megan's clothing or jewelry had ever been found. He'd admitted to all the murders and relished discussing them. The murders were his life's work, and if he'd killed Megan, he would've wanted to take credit for it.

But after two years, Kevin was the closest person to a suspect Tom had, and coming to the prison was a last-ditch effort. And now with no suspects, it was the first time since Megan disappeared that Tom had relinquished all hope she'd be found.

For almost thirty minutes Hannah watched the entrance of The Rusty Nickel. Four men had walked in, and nobody had come out. She had the impression it was the type of joint that if you looked at someone the wrong way, they'd lock the front door and take turns using your face as a punching bag then throw you in the alley like trash. Being a petite female at only five foot five and barely weighing a hundred pounds, she didn't want to think what they could do to her. To say she needed to be vigilant would be an understatement.

Hannah placed a quarter into the payphone and

dialed. No answer. She looked down at her watch—9:13. She'd try again in three minutes.

A man walked out of The Rusty Nickel and leaned against the brick wall and lit a cigarette. Hannah watched him for a long moment, then a snowplow sped east on Colfax and obstructed her view. The engine roared, becoming almost deafening as sparks shot up like fireworks where the plow and the pavement met. After the plow passed, the man was gone and the sidewalk was deserted.

She looked down at her watch—9:16. She tapped on the receiver, then placed a quarter in the slot and dialed. It rang four times before the answering machine message played.

"It's Hannah. I've found Ben—or well, I think I've found him. At The Rusty Nickel off Colfax and Federal. And I'm going to try to get him to talk. I'll call you in the morning, by seven, and if you don't hear from me, I'm in trouble, and you should come looking for me. He's staying at the Lakewood Motel, room number seven. Wish me luck."

Hannah hung up the phone then opened her purse and pulled out cherry-red lipstick and a compact. After touching up her makeup, she took a quick, shallow breath then dashed across Colfax.

In the bar, Hannah walked straight to the jukebox. She inserted a dollar and browsed all of the albums before finally selecting three songs. Then she made her way to the bar top, sitting two stools to Ben's left. A few minutes later, the bartender walked over and she ordered a vodka soda.

Hannah sipped on the drink, chewing on a piece of gum and blowing the occasional bubble. She glanced at the TV above the bar, where the Nuggets were playing the Lakers. "About a Girl" by Nirvana started blaring from the blown-out speakers. She turned to Ben, made eye contact, and smiled. Don't stare too long—don't ever stare too long.

"Nice song selection," the man said.

Hannah turned and blew a bubble. She waited for it to pop, then said, "What?"

"I said nice song selection—most of the drunks in here play country shit that makes you want to blow your brains out."

"Thanks, I guess."

"I'm just telling it like it is." He moved into the barstool next to Hannah. "I'm Charles," he said.

Not the slightest bit of hesitation in lying about his name. He probably did it so often that it was second nature.

"Hello Charles, I'm Tiffany," Hannah said.

"It's nice to meet you."

She nodded, smiled, and blew a bubble.

"So, what brings you to this fine establishment?" he said.

"Are you referring to this shithole?"

"I like to say it's a dive bar with a touch of charisma and character. I mean, who doesn't like people doing blow in every booth and puke on the bathroom floor?"

"To each their own," she said, raising her glass.

"But really, what brings you here?"

"I have twenty dollars and need to get fucked up, and this place looks like I can accomplish my goal on that budget."

"Well, you picked the right place. I don't think there's another bar in town where you can get a PBR and a shot of Beam for five dollars," he said pointing to the specials chalkboard behind the bar.

"I'm more of a vodka girl," she said with a smile and a wink.

Flirting with him made her queasy, but if she wanted answers, she'd have to fake interest until she was alone with him. "So, tell me about yourself," Hannah said, placing her hand on his thigh.

She laughed at his dumb jokes, played with her hair, touched his arms more times than she liked—a checklist from a "How to Show Him You're Interested" article in Vogue.

At one point in the conversation, Hannah lied and said she'd just gotten back from Las Vegas and asked if he'd ever been. He told her he'd never been west of Grand Junction. Hannah knew that was a lie. She had a knack for spotting liars. The look in a person's eyes was all she needed, like a professional poker player observing tells of weaker opponents.

On two occasions, Hannah slipped into the bathroom and poured out the vodka drink into the sink, refilling it with water. Being alone with this man was dangerous, but being alone with him and being inebriated could be deadly.

"Okay, what is the best concert you've seen? And if your answer sucks, I don't know if we can still be friends," Hannah said with a giggle.

"Fuck, that's a tough one."

"Come on, it's easy. Best show you've seen."

"I'm going to go with the Guns N' Roses and Metallica show at Mile High. Metallica was fucking amazing and then G N' R came on, and Axel got pissed about something and stormed off the stage after the first song. Then like thirty minutes later, he walks back out and finishes the set. I heard a rumor that the promoter pulled a gun on him and forced him to go back on stage. Crazy shit."

"I think I can accept that answer," Hannah said.

"Damn straight you will! What about you?"

"Easy, Nine Inch Nails and David Bowie at McNichols. I took a handful of mushrooms before the show, and when the lights went out for Bowie I was on another planet. I don't even remember moving for the entire show. Then, after it was over, I sat with my boyfriend in the bed of his truck and stared up at the stars. It was a life-changing experience," Hannah said, occasionally drumming on the bar rail.

"That sounds fucking amazing!"

"Last call for alcohol," the bartender yelled to the few remaining patrons. "You don't have to go home," he continued. "But you can't stay here," some drunkards yelled, joining the bartender.

"So, what's your plans for the rest of the night?" he said.

"I'm open for anything," Hannah said with a touch of seduction.

"I have a room like six blocks away. It's kind of a shithole, but I have booze and some party favors."

"Let's go."

Twenty minutes later, Hannah was staring into the mirror above the sink in the tiny bathroom of room number seven at the Lakewood Motel. She was anxious, but confident, and as long as she kept him on the bed, everything should go to plan.

She turned on the sink, cupped her hands, and slurped some water. Then she flung her purse over her shoulder, removed her gun, and swung open the bathroom door.

He sprang up onto the bed, moments away from charging her.

"Don't take another step," she said pointing the gun at him.

"What the—" he muttered, his eyes never leaving the weapon.

"Strip to your underwear and put these on," Hannah said.

She tossed two pairs of PlastiCuffs onto the bed. He looked down at them then back at her.

"What the fuck is going on?"

"I need some information from you, but before we start, you're going to put a pair of those around your ankles and tighten them, then you'll roll onto your stomach and slide the other pair around your wrists. Then I'll come over and cinch them nice and tight. It's just a safety precaution so nobody gets hurts—mostly you, since I'm the one holding the gun."

He stared at her with dead eyes and clenched fists, his lips twitching with every breath.

"I know you're calculating if you can jump off the bed and get to me before I can get off a shot. Trust me when I say this. I can, and I will, shoot out your kneecap before you make it two steps, and I promise that's not how you want to spend the rest of the night."

"What the fuck do you want?"

"I just want to have a conversation with you, Ben," she said.

His eyes shifted, and he became tense.

"Yes, I know you're Benjamin Paterson, and I know what you did in Vegas, and we're going to talk about that later, but first, please take off your clothes and put the cuffs on so we can get started."

Hannah leaned against the wall, watching his every move, with the barrel pointed directly at him. The room became quiet, and for a few moments she thought he might make the gamble and charge her, but eventually he lowered his head, pulled off his T-shirt, and unbuttoned his pants. They dropped to the floor, and he kicked them to Hannah's feet.

The man sat at the edge of the bed and cuffed his ankles, then rolled onto his stomach and wrapped his left wrist, pulling it tight. He slid his right hand through the opening before turning to Hannah. She instructed him to roll onto his back. He complied. Finally, she could let out a silent sigh of relief, knowing she was 100 percent in control.

She smiled and nodded. "See, if you do what I say, I'll be gone before you know it."

Grabbing the desk chair, she moved it toward the bed, sitting in it backward. She lit a cigarette, took a drag, and watched the smoke clouds escape her lips.

"Tell me about Megan Floyd."

"I don't know a Megan Floyd."

"I know you know her, and I also know you guys worked together in Fraser, so please don't lie to me again."

"I think you've got me confused with someone else."

Hannah held her breath fleetingly, looking up at the yellowish ceiling. She felt déjà vu but couldn't pinpoint it. Maybe it was one of the countless men who'd lied to her at some point in her life.

After a few seconds, she leaned over and in a seamless motion jammed the cigarette straight down into his stomach. It sizzled, burning the pale skin and belly hair. Ben let out a cry and squirmed, attempting to turn away from Hannah. She lifted the cigarette and dropped it into the ashtray. The smell of burnt hair and flesh filled the room.

"You fucking bitch!"

"See what happens if you call me a bitch again."

"I'm going to fucking kill you!"

Reaching down she picked up her purse and removed two four-inch trigger clamps, which she dangled in front of the man.

"These, Benjamin, are trigger clamps" She paused momentarily. "And I'm going to place one on each of your testicles and pull the trigger every time I ask a question that you don't answer, or if I think you are lying to me. And for every time you call me a bitch, I'll pull that trigger twice."

He didn't respond.

"I'm pretty sure you don't want this, and I really don't want to do it, I really don't. Getting these on your balls is going to take some work. You're going to fight and flail, and I'm going to have to put out a pack of cigarettes on you, but in the end, I'll get them on. Then do you know what happens?"

He stared at her, vacant faced.

"These little guys might look small, but they produce thirty-five pounds of pressure." She squeezed the trigger. "The first few squeezes will hurt, but after that you'll probably go numb, and maybe not even feel that your balls are being crushed, but I can promise you that when I take them off and all the blood starts rushing back to your testicles, you'll be in the worst pain of your life."

Speechless, the man began rocking on the bed.

"And yelling for help isn't going to do shit. I could yell right now at the top of my lungs that I'm being raped and none of these degenerates at this shithole motel would even care, so I guarantee they're not going to give two fucks about some guy yelling for help. They'll probably just think it's some BDSM shit."

Hannah paused, then gracefully leaned back and started playing with her hair. She could see in his eyes that he'd conceded—it was only a matter of time before she started getting answers.

"Now, are you ready to talk?"

"Ask your fucking questions," he said under his breath.

"Let's start from the beginning. Are you Benjamin Henry Paterson?"

He nodded.

"Do you mind if I call you Ben?"

"I don't care what you fucking call me."

"Perfect. Tell me about your relationship with Megan Floyd," Hannah said, resting her elbows on top of the chair.

He coughed, then cleared his throat. "We were friends and hung out, nothing more, nothing less."

"Define hung out."

"We'd get fucked up together, okay? Two, three times a week. Weed, acid, coke—but mostly meth. She loved crystal."

"Your drugs or hers?"

"Mostly hers."

An argument started in the adjacent room—they both looked at the wall, then back at each other.

"Who was she buying from?"

Ben shrugged. "I don't remember his name."

Hannah sat up in the chair. "I don't believe about half the shit that comes out of your mouth, and I think you might have had something to do with Megan's disappearance. Otherwise, you wouldn't be lying to me right now."

"I swear I didn't! We were friends."

"Then tell me the fucking truth!"

"She was getting her shit from this guy named Nathan. I, umm, I only met him a couple of times. I always got a bad vibe from him. He seemed like one of those guys that can snap at any moment and completely lose it, you know? And I didn't want to be around when it happened."

"Keep going," Hannah said, gesturing with one of the clamps.

"Well, like three weeks before she went missing, she came back from his house, and something had happened. Like she looked terrified, I could see the fear in her eyes. I asked what happened, but she didn't want to talk about it. And then when she went missing, I knew that dude probably had something to do with it."

"And you never thought about telling the police this information?"

"Seriously, and put a spotlight on me? You're fucking crazy. They had zero fucking suspects, and I was a close friend, who happened to be a fucking junkie. I would've never made it out of the interrogation room. Fuck, they still don't have any idea who did it."

Hannah stared for a moment, then said, "Would you happen to know Nathan's last name?"

He chuckled. "You think I have the last name of some drug dealer? No, I fucking don't. But next time I'll ask for his full name and social security number."

"Have you seen him since Megan disappeared?"

"I don't think so—well, maybe. I coulda swore someone was following me a couple nights after she went missing. I was walking to a friend's house in Baker and had the feeling that I was being followed, so I made a detour and cut up a couple alleys and looped back up around and the guy was still following. I finally turned around and yelled, "Fuck you, cocksucker," and then I saw him pull out a gun. I turned and bolted faster than I've ever run. I was like a chicken with its head cut off. After a few minutes, I jumped into someone's patio and hid there for like an hour."

He looked down at his stomach. The burn was fire-red and starting to blister.

"You think it was Nathan?"

"I don't know. He never got closer than like forty or fifty feet, so I only saw a silhouette. For all I know, it could've been someone trying to rob me, but it scared the shit out of me so I said fuck it, better safe than sorry. I packed up and moved to Vegas like two weeks later."

"And the situation with Molly is why you came back to Denver," Hannah said.

"I didn't really have anywhere else to go. I figured if I kept a very low profile, I would be good."

"I found you in less than three days, so you're not keeping that low of a profile."

He looked at her with a face that said "fuck you."

"You said you'd met Nathan a couple of times. Where?"

"I don't remember. I was blasted every time."

She stared at him for a long moment, tapping on the chair.

"I'm only going to ask one more time. Where did you meet Nathan?"

"It was at this car audio store in Lakewood off of Colfax and Kipling. I think it's called 5280 Car Audio or something like that. It's owned by Nathan's partner. It's a real audio business, but they deal dope out of the back door so it's an awesome front. His name was Chris, or Cory, something like that."

Hannah was confident that he was finally being truthful. "See, was that so hard?"

"That's all I know, I fucking promise!"

"I know, Ben, and I'd like to thank you for your cooperation, but I must get going," she said, reaching for the phone.

"Get these fucking things off me!"

"I'm sorry, I can't do that."

"Wait, I thought if I answered your questions, you'd let me go."

Hannah leaned toward the bed and whispered, "Did you really think I'd let you go free after what you did in Las Vegas? You must be dumber than I thought."

Ben spit on her forehead, some of it landing in her eyes.

"You little fucking cunt, I'm going to skull fuck you!"

She wiped away the saliva with the front of her hand, then smeared it on the bedsheets.

"Enjoy your next few years behind bars, you piece of shit."

Hannah picked up the phone and started to dial the Denver County sheriff.

Sitting at the bar, Tom stared into his half-empty pint glass, slowly moving his fingers across the grooves in the warped wood. A group of guys were playing pool in the back, betting a pitcher of beer on every game. Tom suspected they were prison guards—work, go to the bar, get drunk, and go home, and repeat almost daily. He knew that pattern all too well.

"What's your name?" a woman said two barstools to his left. She was probably twenty-five, maybe thirty, and pretty. She would've been a five out of ten in Denver, but she was a nine in this podunk town, and probably harassed daily.

Tom looked around and pointed to himself.

"Yes, you. I'm Becky. What can I call you?

"I'm Tom."

She smiled. "Very nice to meet you, Tom. I don't think I've seen you in here before?"

"It's because I've never been here before. I should be somewhere around Idaho Springs, but since 25 is still closed, I had to get a room, and I needed a drink so I walked down here."

"I bet when you woke up this morning you never thought you'd be sitting in this bar, on this barstool, at this very moment."

"I did not."

"Fate is funny like that huh? A perfect example is my last relationship. I won't bore you with minutiae, but I met him at a concert, a local metal band that you've probably never heard of. I always think about what would've happened if I would've stayed home that night instead of going. I probably would've never met him, and the next three years of my life would've been utterly different. And even if I would've met him weeks, or maybe even months later, I could've been dating someone, or he could've been dating someone, or whatever other countless scenarios that could've been in play."

Tom looked in the beer, then took a drink. It'd been a long day, and all he wanted was to get drunk alone, not conversation. He briefly considered asking her to leave.

She continued, "By deciding to go to that show that night, my life went down path A instead of going down path B."

"I can think of countless choices that brought me here tonight, and none of them for the better," Tom said.

"I'd love to know why you're here."

"The prison."

"I should've figured. Are you a cop or something?"

"Used to be in my previous life."

"What do you do now?"

"I'm still trying to figure that out."

Becky hopped into the barstool next to Tom. "So, how'd it go?" she whispered.

"The visit to the prison? Not as well as I'd hoped."

"Would you care to elaborate?"

"Let's just say I didn't get the answers I was searching for."

"Did you ask the right questions?"

He paused again, looking at her sideways. "I honestly don't know anymore."

"I can't sit here and let you be down in the dumps, so this is what we're going to do. I'm going to buy us a shot of whiskey, and then we will do said shot, and then we will gauge how you're feeling. If you're still down, a second or third shot might be necessary. But for starters, you're sitting next to me, so at a minimum there should be a smile on your face," Becky said, placing her hand on his back.

He smiled. "Thanks for the offer, but I probably should head back to my room after this drink. I gotta be up early so I can be on the road when they open 25 back up."

She stared at him and took a drink, followed by about twenty seconds of awkward silence. "You're not very good at this, are you?" she asked.

"Good at what?"

"Flirting. I've been trying to hit on you for the last few minutes."

Tom turned red. "I'm so sorry, I thought you were just being friendly."

It'd been years since he'd been hit on, so long that he forgot what it felt like. Suddenly he became nervous, like a teenage boy asking his crush to the school dance.

"And I should tell you that I'm married," he blurted.

"Oh, you're married? No ring though."

Tom looked down at his hand. "I didn't even realize I wasn't wearing it."

Becky nodded.

"You're very pretty, and I'd love to ask you back into my room and spend the night with you, but I still love my wife and don't think I could live with myself if I did."

He was taken aback that he'd been that blunt. The longer Megan was missing, the further apart he and Lisa drifted.

"I understand, and I respect that, but if I'm being honest, you just missed out on an amazing night." Becky kissed Tom on the cheek, then whispered, "I hope you find the answers you're looking for."

Tom watched her walk to the pool tables, second-guessing his decision to be honest the entire time.

Twenty-five minutes later, he was back in the hotel room, alone. Sitting on the edge of the bed, he turned on the TV and started flipping through channels. After a couple minutes of channel surfing, he stopped on Colorado Springs Channel 5's ten o'clock news. The weatherman proclaimed that this was a once-in-a-decade storm that seemly occurred every other year. Tom tossed the remote over his shoulder and dropped back into the bed.

"She's not worth it," he whispered. "Just jerk off and go to bed. Nothing good will happen if you go back there."

He reached for the Bud Light on the nightstand, but the can was practically empty, so he set it back down. He thought about the last time he'd had sex with Lisa. It'd been over a year, and that was the first and only time since Megan went missing.

For a few brief weeks, they'd attempted to resume a normal life—going to dinner and the movies, nights out in Denver, meeting up with friends, a weekend ski getaway to Crested Butte, ultimately with a goal of rekindling a sexual relationship.

One night they went out to dinner and Lisa started drinking practically the moment they sat down. She'd finished three glasses of wine before dinner arrived, and continued drinking throughout the meal, barely touching her eggplant parmesan.

When they arrived home, Lisa pushed him onto the couch and started kissing him passionately. Within minutes they made their way into the bedroom, shedding pieces of clothing along the way, and after a brief period of foreplay, they started to have sex, but almost immediately

Lisa started crying. She yelled at him to get off, and before Tom could react, she slapped him in the face, giving him a black eye that remained for three days.

To his best recollection, they hadn't even kissed since that night.

Sometime during Jay Leno, he climbed out of bed and walked over to the window, peering through the blinds. For the first time in about twenty-four hours, the snow had stopped.

Shifting to his left, he stared at the flashing "Open" sign above the door. He remained there, motionless, for a long time. Finally, Tom bent down, put on his boots, and walked out of the room.

He stopped at the bar door. If he went back to his room, his life would continue down the same trajectory, for better or for worse, but if he walked into the bar, his life with Lisa was over, and he knew it. The longer he stood there, the harder the decision became. He felt like he was on the verge of a mental breakdown.

"Fuck it," Tom said, pulling the door open.

There was no sign of Becky inside, and after a moment he flagged the bartender to come over.

"Remember me from earlier? I was sitting over there and talking to this girl."

"Yeah, that was Becky."

"Yes! Do you know if she's still here?"

"No," the man said, shaking his head. "I think she left with some guy like twenty minutes ago."

Tom thanked the bartender, then walked to the room, kicked off his boots, and lay down in the bed. Another night alone.

FOUR

Hannah slipped into her apartment, then slammed the door behind her and turned the deadbolt. She paused for a moment before running into the bathroom and dropping to her knees on the toilet mat, clutching the bowl. The porcelain was cold against her skin.

Being alone in the motel room with Ben had scared her. One misstep and he could've taken control of the situation, and she could've easily ended up dead in a dumpster. And being scared is how you make a mistake, and that made her question if she was meant for this type of work. She felt ill, and she needed a release.

Extending her middle finger, she slowly slid it down her throat until it reached the esophagus, then began tickling it. Not being a novice, she knew exactly how to trigger the gag reflex. Shortly after she began a series of dry heaves, but continued working the back of her throat until a steady stream of mostly clear liquid gushed from her mouth.

Nearly a minute later, she sat back onto her heels and stared up into the mirror. She was white as a ghost, and beads of sweat dotted her forehead. A mixture of saliva and bile congealed on the corner of her lips. She wiped it with the back of her hand, then lowered herself down to the linoleum and closed her eyes.

While on the floor, she felt the urge to cut herself. It'd been sixty-eight days since a razor blade sliced open her flesh, and she'd thought the cravings were gone, but like placing a bottle in front of an alcoholic, she was no match for the urges. Euphoria rushed throughout her entire body with the thought of cutting herself.

Hannah stood up, walked into the bedroom, slipped off her pants, and slipped into bed. Reaching over, she opened the top drawer of the nightstand and rummaged around the contents until she located a new razor blade toward the bottom of the drawer. She ripped off the protective cardboard casing and brought the blade to her lips.

Slowly, she moved the blade down across her body until it was against her upper right thigh. Her breathing was heavy, almost orgasmic. She pressed the blade, about an eighth of an inch, into her thigh, then meticulously pulled it up against her pale skin. Blood started rushing down her thigh, drowning the bedsheets.

After a long moment, Hannah removed the blade and placed it on the nightstand. Then she began rubbing the blood into her thighs.

Sixty-eight days to zero.

Driving north on Highway 40 through Winter Park, Tom saw something in his peripheral vision that caught his attention. Ignoring traffic laws, he made a U-turn across a double yellow and turned into the Trailhead Inn parking lot. Pulling into a parking spot in front of the lobby, he turned off the 4Runner and stared into the rearview mirror.

This was the moment he knew one day he'd have to face. The random callers hanging up, the rumors about her infidelity, the disappearing for days on end with blatant lies explaining her absence. And she always came home reeking of perfume, as if trying to cover up something or someone.

After some time, he stepped out and walked across the nearly empty parking lot to the maroon Ford Explorer with "WP", "BRK" and "VAIL" bumper stickers on the back window. The license plate confirmed what he already knew—it was her car. He placed his hand on the hood, cold as the day. Defeated, he leaned back and looked up to the gradient gray sky.

"Lisa, Lisa, Lisa," he muttered.

Tom kicked the front tire a few times and contemplated his two choices: continue home and pretend like he never saw her car, and keep hoping that somehow their marriage could be fixed, or confront Lisa, and get resolution today.

He remained there for a long time.

Finally, he walked to room Number Two, the door directly in front of the Explorer. He placed his ear against the wood and listened. Nothing but the TV. Tom placed his thumb over the peephole and knocked three times. No response. He knocked again, this time louder.

"We don't need housekeeping today," a man's voice said.

Tom banged the door with the bottom of his fist. He waited about ten seconds, then banged again. The curtain moved, but then nothing.

"I'm not going anywhere. I've got all day," Tom said.

"Back away and I'll come outside," Lisa said.

Tom removed his finger and stepped back to the open parking spot next to the Explorer. The door crept open about twenty inches, and Lisa squeezed through before shutting it behind her. She stared at Tom vacantly. Her eyes told him everything.

"What are you doing here?" he said.

"Go home."

Tom took a deep breath, gazing at the faded parking lines. "Who is he?"

"Does it matter?"

"Yeah, it does!"

She turned and pointed to the hotel door. "No, it doesn't, but if you must know, he's just some random guy. I don't even know his last name. Honestly, I couldn't care who it was as long as it wasn't you."

He looked at her, then looked away.

"You're starting to hate me as much as I hate you. That's good—we should hate each other. I really don't see any other way to end this nightmare," Lisa said.

"I'll never hate you."

"Well maybe you should—it'd be better for the both of us."

"Just give me a little more time to fix this," Tom pleaded.

"You can't. It's been over for a long time, and you're the only one who doesn't realize it. Do you think that if you found whoever murdered Megan, we miraculously would go back to a normal life? Do you really think that? I know you're not that dumb."

Tom was at a loss for words.

She walked toward him and lightly tapped her fist on his chest. "I'm fucking dead inside. And I fucked that guy in there to see if I could feel something, anything. I don't know what else to do. I'm so close to the edge, so fucking close," Lisa said.

The tapping quickly turned into open-fist punches, and the punches increased in speed and velocity. Tom stood like a statue, chest forward, taking punch after punch after punch. Five, ten, twenty. Finally, she stopped, almost falling over from exhaustion. After a long, deep breath, she looked up at him with tears rushing down her face.

"I'm sorry, I'm sorry," Lisa whispered as she turned back to the room.

Tom took one step forward, then stopped. Up to that point, he'd held on to the smallest chance that the marriage could be salvaged, but now he knew it was over. There was nothing he could say or do to mend the damage that had been done.

Paralyzed, he watched Lisa walk back into the motel room, and perhaps out of his life forever.

Hannah wasn't sure why she came to these meetings— probably some masochism component in her fucked-up brain. Listening to strangers discuss the worst day of their life didn't aid her sorrow, but it did make her realize how much she missed her sister. On good days, what happened to Casey would escape from her consciousness, but walking into this room always brought the memories back to the forefront.

"Brittany was my baby, my only kid. I never really pictured myself as a dad, and by the time I hit my thirties I thought having a kid was out of the picture, but then I met Sarah and we pretty much fell in love overnight. Sarah was pregnant about six months later," the man across from Hannah said.

The man paused and looked down at the checker tiles, seemingly searching for his next words. Hannah stared at him for a moment, then nervously looked away and silently brought her legs up and crossed them under her. She tried to remember his name but couldn't. Another nameless stranger.

The man was sitting in a folding chair in a conference room with nine people in a circle. Some of them were watching the man, while others had their heads down or their eyes closed.

Hannah recognized the middle-aged woman directly across from her. They made eye contact, acknowledged each other with a nod, then looked away.

The man continued, "The moment she was born, I knew I'd never love someone as much as I did her. I always thought it was bullshit when parents told me stuff like that, but it's true. You can't really explain it unless you're a parent."

He paused for a moment. Then his eyes searched the room, looking for someone to help.

"She was twelve, almost thirteen, and wanted to spend a month of summer break with her grandma in Salt Lake City. She was scared to death of flying and begged me to take the bus. I was a little concerned, but she was mature for her age, so I agreed. We drove to the bus station, and I walked her to the terminal, and hugged her, and told her I loved her."

Hannah leaned back into the chair and allowed her mind to drift. Listening to these stories always gave her an ugly feeling.

"The driver mixed up his medication and fell asleep at the wheel seven miles outside of Green River, Utah. The bus veered off the highway and landed in a gully, and Brittany was thrown almost two hundred feet from the crash site."

It wasn't that Hannah lacked compassion, it was the opposite. She didn't want to create a personal relationship with any of these people because she would've become obsessed with their tragedies as much as they were. There'd be conversations after meetings, phone call check-ins, weekly lunches, and she'd probably end up going to church with them. It was all part of her obsessive mentality.

Like last summer, when she read *Cadillac Desert*, a book about the depleting Colorado River and the impending drought in the southwest. In an effort to conserve water, she didn't shower for two weeks. Finally, she concluded that she alone couldn't fix the water scarcity in the Southwest, and she gave up and resumed showering daily.

For Hannah, it was easier consciously to ignore their voices, in one ear and out the other.

"But she was a fighter and made it back to the hospital in Grand Junction. The doctors did all they could, but her injuries were too much to overcome, and she passed that next day."

The man dropped his head and rubbed his eyes for a moment, then motioned with his other hand that he was finished.

"Thank you so much for sharing, Doug," said the counselor.

There was light clapping and a hushed "thank you" from the room.

The counselor turned to Hannah. "Hannah, would you like to share anything with the group?"

She sat motionless for a quick moment, then nodded without making eye contact with anyone in the room. This was the part she hated, but she knew she had to. Talking to strangers about Casey was her way of keeping her sister alive.

"I was fifteen and living with my mom and dad in Fort

Collins. My sister Casey was four years older than me and living up in Laramie, going to the University of Wyoming and majoring in Agriculture."

Hannah smiled. Then it quickly disappeared. She tried to sound strong, but her voice was thin, hollow. It always was when she spoke about Casey.

"We had this dream of opening a plant store after I graduated college. She was going to run the agriculture side, and I was going to run the business side. We even had a name for it—CH Plants and Stuff. We were going to specialize in rare and hard-to-find houseplants." Hannah paused for a moment. "Even as a stupid teenager, I knew it was farfetched, and probably never going to happen, but that didn't stop me from doodling logos when I should've been doing homework."

Her right knee was bobbing, and her heart was racing. It didn't matter how many times she told the story. It never got easier. Never.

"The last time we talked was Friday, January 20, 1989. I was planning to stay the weekend at her apartment, but a storm rolled in and my dad didn't want to drive me up there, then drive home, and then pick me up two days later, so we pushed the sleepover to the following weekend. That night we talked on the phone until about six. Nothing important. Just teenage girl drama, boys, friends, school. She was such a good listener. After about forty minutes, I had to get ready for dinner and we said our goodbyes. The last thing she said to me was 'Talk to you later, butthead.'"

Hannah bent down and grabbed a cup of water. After taking a sip, she gently placed the cup back onto the floor.

"That night, someone jimmied her patio door, snuck into her bedroom, bound her to her bed, and proceeded to repeatedly rape her for the next few hours. He stopped at some point to make a sandwich and eat a couple of Oreos. And before he left, he stabbed her multiple times in the stomach and chest with a steak knife, and just left her there to die. She bled out for hours, probably going in and out of consciousness, dying sometime that morning."

She paused. The furnace kicked on, and everyone except Hannah flinched and momentarily turned to it.

"To this day, it's still an unsolved homicide. Ten years, and he is still out there."

Another seven people spoke, but all of them were in one ear and out the other. The counselor provided his final thoughts, then thanked everyone, and before he finished his last words, Hannah had both feet on the floor, speeding to the exit.

Forty minutes later, she was standing on the front porch of her father's duplex, holding a grocery store bouquet, an assortment of sunflowers, daisies, snapdragons, and lilies. A stray cat began walking toward her, but disappeared into a shrub when a car backfired in the alley.

Hannah pressed the doorbell and took a step back. She always worried her father wouldn't answer. That he'd had a heart attack and was dead on the other side of the door.

He was fifty-nine, a lifelong smoker and heavy drinker, and currently battling prostate cancer. And besides Hannah, he didn't have anyone else in his life. The friends he'd had either passed, moved away, or were dealing with their own health issues. And his immediate family had all passed as well. Both parents had died in 1989 three months apart, and his only brother died in a drunk driving accident a few years back. Being alone was a symptom of growing old.

For Hannah, her dad was the only family she had left. Technically, she had some cousins in one of the Carolinas and an aunt and uncle on her mother's side, but Hannah hadn't talked to them in nearly a decade. And there was her mother, but she was more of an acquaintance than a parent. Someone who calls on birthdays and sends a Christmas card with fifty dollars, more out of guilt than love.

They only had each other. Thoughts of her dad dead on the kitchen floor kept Hannah up at night, and she made a routine of visiting him every few days.

After about twenty long seconds, the door slowly began to open.

"Hannah!"

"Hi Dad," Hannah said, extending the bouquet.

"What are these for? Did I forget my birthday again?"

"No, it's your one-year anniversary."

"It's been a year already? It feels like yesterday I was getting chemo injections every goddamn day and throwing up every night."

He looked frail, probably down twenty pounds in the last few months. That worried her.

"Well, they worked, right?" she said.

"Yeah, yeah." He looked at the flowers. "What am I supposed to do with those?"

"Do you have a vase?"

"Maybe, I don't know. I know I've got an empty spaghetti jar that I've been keeping weed in, but I haven't had any of that in months, so I guess I could use it for these."

Hannah hugged him hard, then stepped into the house. The place was in disarray—it always was. Fast-food containers, old newspapers, junk mail, empty cigarette packs, and overfilled ashtrays on almost every flat surface.

Hannah found a vase under the kitchen sink and filled it with water, then cut the stems and placed the flowers in. She began arranging the flowers, then placed the vase in the middle of the kitchen table. After admiring it for a moment, she began cleaning the kitchen.

"You don't have to do that—the maid should be here tomorrow."

Hannah smiled. "My ass you have a maid." She dumped an ashtray into the trash can and turned to him. "I thought your doctor asked you to quit smoking."

"He asked, and I listened, thought about it, then I said no."

"Did you at least cut back?"

"Yes, I'm down to a pack a day."

She glared at him.

"I'm only kidding, honey. You really need to learn how to take a joke."

Hannah wiped down the table and put some dishes into the dishwasher. When she was finished, she walked into the living room and sat on the couch.

"How are you really doing?" she said, placing a hand on his knee.

"I'm okay, still chugging along, I guess. And I've been playing those scratch tickets down at the corner store and won twenty dollars, so there's that."

"How much did you spend before you won that twenty dollars?"

"I'm sorry, but that's confidential," he said.

They talked for the next few minutes, mostly about Hannah—her work, her cases, her nonexistent dating life.

"Have you heard from your mom?" he said.

"Not since the obligatory birthday call. I'd say I've talked to her for about a total of fifteen minutes in the last couple of years. I'm a distant memory of a different life, and I don't really blame her. She has her dream life, you know—the lawyer husband and his two smart, beautiful children and that six-room mansion in Cherry Hills. I'm the last remaining link to her previous life, and I'm sure she would be okay if we never talked again."

"I'm sorry, honey. I still love you more than anything."

"Thanks, Pop. I'd actually be okay if I didn't talk to her again either." She paused. "I've always been a daddy's girl anyways."

Her dad smiled. They relaxed into the couch and turned on the TV.

After some time, Hannah looked at him and said, "Do you ever think you'd still be with Mom if Casey was alive?"

"God no! I'd fallen out of love with her long ago and was just holding out until you went off to college. It wasn't Casey's fault, or your fault—the marriage had just run its course, and what happened to Casey just pushed the timeline up a couple of years."

"In two weeks it'll be nine years."

He sighed. "I know, I know. I think about her every goddamn day and miss her more than the last. I sometimes wished the cancer would've gotten me so I could be with her, but then you'd be alone."

Hannah thought about that for a moment, unsure how to respond. Unbeknownst to her father, she reciprocated the feeling, having contemplated suicide numerous times, but thoughts of leaving him alone always stopped her.

She opened her arms and hugged him for a long time.

Following his visit with Kevin, Tom needed someone to talk to. After considering the few people he was still in communication with, he decided to call Marshall. They agreed to meet at Marshall's office the following night.

Tom arrived five minutes early. The door to the office was open, and Tom stood in the entrance. Marshall was working on a drink and reading a case file. Tom was about to say something when Marshall glanced up and invited him to sit down.

"How are you doing?" Marshall said.

For a moment, Tom considered telling him everything. That his marriage was essentially over, and for the first time since Megan disappeared, he was certain that she was dead and her body would never be found, and the person responsible would never be caught, and he was considering terminating the contract with Marshall because it was an unsolvable case, and that he felt lost and hopeless.

Finally, he muttered, "It wasn't Kevin."

"Let's have a drink."

Marshall opened a drawer and pulled out a bottle of Jack Daniel's, then a second rocks glass. He filled Tom's glass and slid it across the desk.

"I knew it wasn't him, and I could've told you that a hundred times, but no matter what I said, you still would've wanted to talk to him. You wanted him to be the guy so bad that you needed to figure it out on your own," Marshall said.

They continued talking, father to father, cop to cop, broken man to broken man.

After topping the glasses for the third time, Marshall said, "I never understood the guys who could retire as a detective. I saw too many things that no person should ever see, and I always knew I couldn't do it for the long haul. I had a shelf life. I thought ten, maybe fifteen years would be a good run, but then Maggie Freemont got kidnapped, and that destroyed me."

Tom distinctly remembered the girl's abduction. It made the national news cycle, and the parents even appeared on Larry King, begging for her safe return. A five-year-old girl vanishes from her front yard while playing hide-

and-go-seek with her little brother. The only description the brother could provide was that abductor was a tall Caucasian male with long brown hair. There were no other witnesses. Nobody saw him or Maggie, or his car. It was like he was a ghost.

"Every agency in Denver was looking for her, but after forty-eight hours we had no clues or suspects. Just a long list of maybes, what-ifs, and dead-ends. I was losing hope and began preparing myself for the worst. Then, on the third night, a call came in from a couple that were hiking up on Lookout. Before they left, the girlfriend went to use the pit toilet, and when she walked in, she heard something and yelled for her boyfriend to grab a flashlight. They shined the light into the toilet, and at the bottom of the pit they saw the face of the missing girl, submerged up to her shoulders in human shit."

Marshall paused. He picked up his glass, held it an inch from his face, then gently put it back down on the desk without taking a drink.

"That next morning, Maggie was able to provide us with a description of him, his car, and a partial license plate. We were at his front door two hours later, and that motherfucker was in jail that night. Seeing him in that jail cell was the proudest moment of my life."

Tom thought about what it must've felt like to rescue the girl and catch the man who did it. Probably close to the feeling he'd get if he solved Megan's disappearance.

"He was sentenced to twenty years, but released after six for good behavior. The parole board deemed he was safe to return to society. Six fucking years is all the time that that piece of shit got for destroying that little girl's life. Six fucking years."

Marshall turned then coughed into his fist.

"After he was released, he moved in with his mom into

her doublewide in Sheridan. Then he got a job at a gas station working graveyards, and pretty much returned to a normal life. I vowed to myself that he'd never hurt another kid again. He became an obsession. I'd park in front of that mobile home for hours at a time, just waiting for the right moment. I started to have these visions of kicking in the front door and jamming the barrel of my gun down his throat and pulling the trigger. I started to convince myself I could trade his life for a life in prison.

"Then my wife told me she was going to leave me if I didn't stop, so I did. And then three months later, he kidnapped a seven-year-old girl from the mobile home park and strangled the kid to death, leaving her body in a trash can. He died in a police shootout later that night."

Tom felt ill. He knew about Maggie Freemont's kidnapper being caught and being sentenced to twenty years. That had made the local news and front page of both Denver papers, but he had no idea the kidnapper had been released. He wanted to say something, but knew anything he could say wouldn't matter, so he leaned back and sipped on the whiskey.

There was a long silence, then Marshall said, "I should've just kicked in the fucking door. He couldn't have killed that kid if I'd just kicked in the damn door. And not doing it really fucked me up. I couldn't sleep for a long time. I'd lay in bed and just stare at the ceiling for hours. I was living some nightmare, neither asleep nor awake. It took a toll on me. I quit the force three months later, then became the stereotypical ex-cop alcoholic, and then my wife left me, and took my daughter with. It ruined my life, along with countless others."

Marshall picked up the glass and finished the whiskey in two gulps. Then he gently placed it back on the desk and looked up at Tom.

"I was dead for a long time, uncertain how to move forward. But after a couple years of a nomadic lifestyle, I somewhat cleared my head and decided to move back to Denver and start the PI firm. I wasn't sure if I could do this type of work again, but it gave me something," Marshall said.

"What is that?"

"A chance at salvation. Every time I solve a missing person case that's collecting dust in some department basement, I feel a little closer to being normal."

The radio was playing *The Bends* by Radiohead on repeat at a low volume. This was the third time Hannah had heard "High and Dry" since she'd pulled into the parking spot.

Her eyes moved down to the notebook on the steering wheel, and she stared at her writing: "5280 Car Audio." She was almost certain that Ben was telling the truth—most guys would with the threat of their testicles being crushed—but there was a small chance that he was lying.

The store was in a somewhat hidden strip mall a block north of Colfax, sandwiched between a liquor store and a laundromat. Neon paint covered almost every inch of the storefront windows— "Biggest Sale of the Year", "We'll Beat Any Price!", "Free Installations on Select Stereos."

The plan was to go in, make up some bullshit story that she was looking for a new stereo, attempt to get the name of the owner, then leave. Child's play, nothing to worry about.

After a deep breath, she slid her wallet under the driver's seat and turned off the car, then started toward the store.

Hannah soon found herself staring at a wall of about twenty different car stereos with two walls on each side full of speakers of different shapes and sizes. She pressed a few buttons, turning stereos on and off while adjusting volume and settings.

"How can I help you today?" an employee said.

"Honestly, I don't have the first idea of what I'm doing. All I know is the stereo in my car is a piece of you-know-what and I need a new one," she said.

"Well, you came to the right place. Do you have a brand preference and a budget you're looking to stay under?"

"I really don't care about a brand, and my budget is around $200. Is that enough to get something good?"

"Of course. Let me show you some different models in that price range."

The employee presented different stereos from Alpine, JVC, and Pioneer, explaining the pros and cons of each one.

"Which one would you recommend?"

"I'd say go with the Pioneer—it's the most bang for your buck, and that one comes with free installation. So, all in it'll be right around $190."

"Okay, let's go with that. I get paid on Friday and could be here around noon. Does that work?"

"Yes, we should be able to get it installed in about an hour or two."

"Perfect! Thanks for all of your help. I'm Tracy, by the way," Hannah said.

"Nice to meet you, Tracy. I'm Craig, I own the store, so if you need anything, just give me a call and I'll be able to help you out," Craig said, handing her a business card.

Hannah smiled. It wasn't Chris or Cory, but Ben did have the first initial correct.

"Great, see you Friday. Thanks again."

Hannah walked out of the store and across the parking lot. She climbed into her car and stared at the card, flicking it a couple of times before driving away.

Marshall leaned into the coffee table and dumped about half a dozen blue pills out of the prescription bottle. Methodically, he picked up a spoon and gently placed it on top of one of the pills, pressing down until there was a pop. Then he formed a three-inch line with a credit card.

He preferred snorting OxyContin over swallowing or injecting. In his opinion, swallowing didn't provide the same high, and injecting was out of the question given his phobia of needles.

Leisurely, he leaned down and inhaled the entire line in seconds. Marshall fell back into the couch, allowing his eyes to roll back in his head. It was now a matter of moments before he was in his happy place.

Marshall's dealer, Rex, was sitting across from him in a Papasan Chair. On an almost continuous loop, Rex packed a bowl into his multicolored glass pipe, then smoked it, then ashed it. Load, smoke, ash, repeat. When he wasn't smoking, he hummed song melodies, sometimes singing the lyrics, making up a majority of the words.

About five minutes later, Marshall leaned forward. "What do bottles cost again?"

"Eighty bucks," Rex said.

"Eighty? That's twenty more than I paid last time."

"Sorry brother, I wish I could do better, but times are tough. This shit is getting hard to find, so I've had to go outside my usual connections, and with that comes a premium cost."

"Alright, give me three bottles."

That would make seven for the month, and behind his mortgage, it was Marshall's second-highest expense. He knew he couldn't continue on this pace for much longer, and if something didn't change, odds were he'd be dead in the next few years. He'd heard the stories of the overdoses and deaths, and they were becoming more frequent. That worried him, but the addiction outweighed the fear.

Marshall opened his wallet and counted the bills, then set them in a perfect stack and pushed them across the table. Rex counted it four times. Then he picked up a cash box and opened the combination lock, placing the money inside. Then in reverse order, he shut the box, mixed the lock, replaced it on the shelf, and grabbed three prescription bottles without labels, setting them on the table.

"Three, seven, two," Marshall said.

"Huh?" Rex said.

"Three, seven, two. That's the numbers for your cash box. You really did a piss-poor job of concealing the combination from me."

"I, umm, I just figured—I guess I just kinda forgot."

"You should be more conscious of your surroundings. I wasn't even trying to look and could see them clear as day."

Rex stared at Marshall, unsure how to respond. Marshall smiled.

"I mean, you don't have to worry about me, but I'm sure there are some guys that'd love to get their hands on your drug money."

"Yeah, you're probably right."

Marshall grabbed the bottles and slipped them into his coat pocket. He started to get up, then stopped and sat back down.

"Have you ever bought anything from a guy named

Nathan who deals out of Evergreen or Conifer or somewhere from up in that area?"

"Fucking once, and only once."

"Please elaborate," Marshall said, leaning in.

"A friend of a friend of an acquaintance tells me that he knows this guy looking to get rid of a couple sheets of acid for a fucking killer deal."

Rex took a big hit, then slowly exhaled, watching the smoke until it disappeared.

"So, I get in touch with this guy, and we agree to a deal, and he tells me to meet him at this house outside of Evergreen. I get up there and it's this huge house on the side of a mountain, probably miles from the next closest neighbor."

"Was it Nathan's house?"

"No, no. It was some rich kid's place. He was having a party while his parents were in Europe. There was probably like fifty people doing almost every drug you can think of. After asking nearly half the party if they know a Nathan, this girl says she knows where he is and takes me to the basement. We say hello, chit-chat for a few minutes, then as I was about to start talking business his demeanor just flipped."

Rex paused for a moment and looked into the kitchen, then turned back to Marshall.

"He gets up and just starts pacing back and forth, then locked the door and lifted his shirt to reveal a handgun. He was acting like I was there to rob him or something, very fucking paranoid. Then he pulls out the gun and points it at me, and starts this evil fucking laugh. I was about to make a dash for the door when he says he was just messing with me. Then he put the gun away and we did the deal. I didn't want to, but I didn't want to do anything that might set him off. About twenty minutes later, I snuck out the back door and got the fuck out of there. I swear, for a couple of minutes I really thought I was going to die. I almost pissed myself."

Rex took another hit.

"He's a real fucking piece of shit if you ask me, and I can promise you that I'm never, ever doing another fucking drug deal in the mountains again. If I want some dope, I'm getting it from someone in the fucking city. Fuck those mountain people—I'm not about to get offed and buried in some mountain grave."

"Did you ever call him?" Marshall said.

Rex nodded. "He paged me a handful of times, and I stupidly called back. I think he said the number was some gas station payphone."

"Would you happen to still have that number?"

Rex looked like he was thinking for a moment, then grabbed an address book from the bottom shelf of the table and started flipping through the pages.

"Here it is," he said, pointing to a number in the book.

"Can I have it?"

"As long as you don't mention my name, I don't give a fuck. That piece of shit can go straight to fucking hell."

FIVE

Marshall turned off Highway 74 into the Sinclair gas station and parked next to the air machine. The station was empty except for the Ford Bronco parked on the side of the building, probably belonging to the graveyard worker. He walked across the parking lot to the payphone. The number of the phone was written above the keypad. It was the same one Rex had given him.

Leaning against the phone, Marshall studied the parking lot and the highway and the mountains that stretched into the darkness. The only sound was the humming of the gas station sign.

About a mile to the east up 74 was Evergreen Lake. That was where he proposed to his ex-wife during an ice-skating date. After a tense, freezing moment, she said yes, and they got married the following summer. Every December for the first five years of their marriage they'd come back up here and have dinner, then ice skate until the lights were turned off. Then they'd have sex in the freezing car like two teenagers. Being up here with his ex-wife was some of his fondest memories—it'd been almost ten years since he'd been to Evergreen, and now it gave him a bad feeling.

Two bells jingled as he pushed the door open, and music was playing at a low volume from the back room. It took Marshall a couple of seconds to recognize the song "Master of Puppets" by Metallica. A kid, probably not old enough to legally drink, walked out from a back room.

"Evening, sir," he said.

Marshall returned the greeting and proceeded to the candy aisle. He scanned the selection of candy bars, then grabbed a Snickers and walked to the counter.

"Is there going to be anything else tonight?" the kid said.

His eyes were glassed over. He was definitely a stoner, most likely a drinker, but probably not into powders.

"Just this."

The kid rang up the purchase, and Marshall placed a dollar on the counter. He smiled and said, "You like Metallica?"

"Yes, sir, one of my all-time favorite bands."

"Ever seen them live?"

"No, sir, I haven't. I hear they're coming this summer, and if they do, I can guarantee you I'll be one of the first people in line when tickets go on sale."

"I'd highly suggest it. I've seen them seven times, and one of my top three concerts of all time was right after *Kill 'Em All* came out. It was at this tiny club in San Diego, something like twenty people there. And after the show, I ended up partying with the band—fuck, me and James actually ended up drinking until the sun came up in some hotel off the beach."

That was a lie. Marshall believed lying was a skill, like

playing the guitar—the more you did it, the better you became. And he considered himself the Eddie Van Helen of lying.

"God damn, mister! I'd give my right nut to have a beer with them."

"It was pretty fucking amazing. And call me Marshall."

"Nice to meet you, Marshall, I'm Patrick," he said, opening the left side of his jacket and revealing the name tag pinned to his shirt.

"Hello, Patrick. Could I ask you some questions regarding an investigation I'm working?"

"Sure mister, go right ahead."

"How long have you worked here?"

Patrick looked up at the fluorescent lights and started doing the math in his head.

"It'll be two years in April."

"Do you usually work overnights?"

"Yes, sir. I've only worked the graveyard here. I prefer this shift, and nobody else wants it, so I get it by default. I usually work Monday to Friday, with the occasional weekend tossed in."

Marshall pointed to the payphone across the lot. "Do you ever see anyone use that payphone regularly? Someone who uses it multiple times a night?"

"I don't think so. It's pretty slow after eleven, so I'm mostly listening to music or reading a comic book in the back room unless I hear the bells ring."

"Know anyone named Nathan who lives around here?"

"No, sir. I live down in Morrison, so I really don't know anyone around here."

Marshall asked a few more questions, but Patrick provided no substantial answers.

"Thanks for your time, Patrick."

"Sure, anytime. Umm, do you mind if I ask what kind

of case this is for?"

"It's a missing person investigation."

"Oh geez, someone from Evergreen?"

"No, it was a girl from Grand County."

"And you think she used to come in this store?"

"No. Just following up on a lead about someone associated with her who came here from time to time."

"The Nathan guy?"

"Yes, the Nathan guy," Marshall said, nodding.

"Shit, sorry I wasn't more help. Do you have a card or something, so I could get in touch with you if I do see anything?"

"Of course," Marshall said, placing a business card on the counter.

"And I'll definitely keep an eye out for this Nathan guy."

Marshall thanked Patrick, walked out of the store, and started back to his car.

Patrick watched Marshall as he crossed the parking lot and climb into his car. After a minute the headlights came on and the car turned east onto Highway 74, disappearing out of sight. Patrick waved for a moment then slowly turned his hand around and extended his middle finger.

"Fuck you, cocksucker," he said under his breath.

Patrick picked up the phone and dialed.

"Hey, it's Patrick. There was just some guy in the store that was asking about you, and some missing girl."

He leaned against the wall and listened.

"No, not a cop—his card says he's a private investigator from Denver," Patrick said. "Marshall York."

He nodded.

"Of course I didn't, I'm not fucking stupid."

He listened for a minute, then said, "No, he turned back toward Denver, and I haven't seen any cars since."

After a brief pause, he said, "Okay, see you in a minute."

Patrick hung up and began pacing behind the counter.

As Tom turned onto County Road 50, he saw Lisa's car in the driveway. Fleetingly he considered driving past the house and staying at a hotel for a night or two, or maybe ten, but at the last moment, he turned into the driveway.

He turned off the car and sat there for a long time, so long the heat faded and the temperature inside the car dropped to what it was outside.

He'd always been convinced Lisa was his soulmate, and now, as bad as he hated to admit it, he was unsure if that was true. There was a little part of him that wished he'd never have to talk to her again.

Finally, Tom got out of the car and walked into the house.

Lisa stood in front of the fireplace, flipping through a handful of pictures. She looked back at Tom with a lifeless expression. After about ten seconds, she turned back to the fire. The fire felt comforting, and he finally realized how cold he'd gotten in the car.

She placed the stack of pictures onto the mantel, positioning them at an angle against the wall, then rested her hands at her sides, staring at the top picture, motionless.

"There were some really good memories in here," she said without turning around. "I kinda forgot about our trip to the Tetons. I still get a little nervous thinking about that grizzly we saw on the hike around Jenny Lake. I thought those rangers were so full of shit about carrying bear spray."

That trip was the first time he said he loved her, and when he realized he was going to marry her.

"They tried to warn you."

"I know, I know. I was so naive, I thought I knew everything about the world."

They remained silent for a long moment.

"That was our last vacation before Meg was born," Tom said.

"It was."

She picked up the top picture from the mantel, stared at it for a moment, then crumpled and tossed it underhand into the fireplace. The fire consumed the picture, turning it into ash in seconds.

"I wasn't even twenty-one," Lisa said.

"Nope. You had that horrible fake ID that you used all over Jackson."

"That's right. I thought for sure I was going to get caught and go to jail, but it worked at every bar." She paused. "That was the first time I ever drank in a bar, and I was so excited I had three Long Island Iced Teas in like an hour. Then I fell off the barstool and almost knocked myself out."

"And I had to carry you about five blocks back to the hotel room."

"Still to this day, I don't think I've ever thrown up as much as I did that night."

Tom nodded. "I don't think there's many people that have thrown up that much ever."

She looked at him and formed fragments of a smile. "I never told you this story before—in fact, I've never told it to anyone. It was the summer after I graduated high school, and a bunch of my friends planned a week-long camping trip up around Bailey. It was going to be the final party before everyone left for college. We basically just got drunk and hung out on the river. The day before we were supposed to go home, I wanted to go tubing, but everyone else was either over it or too hungover. I finally convinced my friend Jim to go. We jumped into the river, and within minutes Jim was out of sight. I was completely alone when I got tossed off my tube and pulled under by the current."

Lisa paused for a few seconds.

"It kept pulling me under, and the more I fought to get to the surface, the more I went under. I finally slammed into the roots of a tree, and my foot got tangled. I don't know how long I was under at that point, but I really started to panic. I was pulling as hard as I could, but I couldn't get my foot untangled. It was such a weird feeling because when I looked down, the water was so murky I couldn't even see my foot, but when I looked up, the sun was shining down onto the surface of the water. It was somewhat peaceful."

Tom was speechless. In their almost twenty years of marriage, he'd never seen her this vulnerable. She was always the strong one, always.

"I could literally feel my lungs getting full, and I decided I was going to give it one last try, and if that didn't work, I was going to say a little prayer and open my mouth. I pulled as hard as I could, and somehow my foot got out and I was back to the surface within seconds. I flailed to shore and crawled into the sand then threw up probably a gallon of river water before I passed out. I'm not sure how long I was there, but when I made it back to camp, everyone was wasted, and they didn't even know I was gone. They thought I was still sleeping. I went back into my tent and cried for the better part of an hour."

Tom shifted slightly, creaking the floorboards.

"I never really thought about that day until Megan went missing. Now it's something I can't get out of my head." Lisa turned her head slightly. "I wish I would've drowned that day. Then Megan would've never been born," she said, barely able to finish.

"Don't talk like that, Lisa."

Lisa lowered her head and muttered, "I should've died that day."

The house was still for a long time—both were statues, with the only sound coming from their breathing and the crackling of the logs.

After some time, Lisa reached across the mantel and picked up a picture. "This one is from our reception. God, we look so fucking young."

Tom closed his eyes and pictured that day. It was a March wedding, and a week out, the forecast had a blizzard coming in the night before, but two days earlier, the storm weakened into scattered rain showers. That day felt like a lifetime ago.

"I think this picture is right after we snuck away to go fuck in that basement bathroom. I probably had ten people ask where we went. I thought my sex hair was a pretty damn good clue," Lisa said.

"I'm pretty sure half the wedding party knew where we went."

Tom had been so nervous he slammed a half pint of Jack before the ceremony and was worried he'd throw up while reciting his vows.

"This was one of the best days of my life," she said.

"Mine too."

"I was convinced on that day that I couldn't love anyone as much as I loved you, just like right now I'm convinced that I'll never love you again."

They were silent for a long, uncomfortable time.

"Do you think you'll ever be able to have some remnant of a normal life?" Lisa said.

"No," Tom said without hesitation.

"Me neither. I really wish I could tell her how much I love her one last time," she said, her voice weak.

Lisa turned back. The tears were rushing down her face, dripping onto her shirt. They both knew this was the end of their life together. They'd never share another kiss, or lie in the same bed, or tell each other their deepest fears and secrets.

Every so often, something would remind them of their time together—a restaurant, a commercial, a movie, a food, a picture, a smell, a taste, a location—and they'd reminisce for a few minutes, but as the years went on, those memories would become less frequent, until their time together would become a distant myth.

"This wasn't your fault, it really wasn't, but I treated you like it was and I'm sorry. I really am, but my heart is broken, completely broken. I wish I could fix it. I wish you could fix it, but we both know there's a piece missing that'll never make it complete again. And I said and did some things I hate myself for," she muttered.

"Stop, Lisa."

"No, it's true. You should hate me for how I treated you," Lisa said.

"I can't hate you. We were put into a predicament that no parents should ever have to go through. I dealt with it the best way I could, and you did the best you could."

Tom looked at Lisa, and they stared at each other for nearly a minute until she turned away.

"I'm leaving on Sunday," she said.

"Where?"

"California. I'm going to stay with my mom for a

while, and try to piece myself back together." She paused. "And I have no plans of coming back to Colorado."

Tom nodded.

"You should leave too," she added. "This house, this town—the memories are going to destroy you like they destroyed me."

"I'm not leaving until I know what happened to Megan."

"I'm starting to think I don't want to know. If she's never found, I'll always have some hope that she still might be alive somewhere."

Glancing up from the fireplace Lisa turned to Tom, "I'm really going to miss you. Take care of yourself."

Lisa blew a kiss, picked up her purse, and disappeared through the kitchen door.

Hannah parked at the 3900 block of Navajo Street in North Denver in front of a corner liquor store. She studied the Bungalow-style home with the red Ford Bronco in the driveway. The porch light shone, illuminating the driveway, the lawn, and the sidewalk.

She'd followed Craig north onto Kipling from the stereo store, keeping at a distance from his red Bronco, almost losing him twice as he sped in and out of traffic, running multiple yellow lights and breaking numerous traffic violations. Hannah almost hit a pedestrian walking his bike in the crosswalk after running a red light, but she swerved into the left-turn lane at the last moment.

Finally, after thirty minutes of a cat-and-mouse pursuit, he turned into the driveway, and Hannah stopped at a safe distance of a hundred feet. She was confident that her pursuit hadn't been detected.

Hannah pushed in the cigarette lighter and patiently waited for it to pop out. She smoked three cigarettes successively, never taking her eyes off the house. It was two stories, with an oversized porch, a manicured lawn, and a large Sycamore tree in the middle of the yard. She'd expected a run-down house with fading paint and cars parked on the lawn, not one she was jealous of. If he was a big-time drug dealer, he masked it well.

Feeling that someone was staring at her, she glanced at the liquor store. A man stood there next to the entrance, sipping on a bottle in a brown paper bag. They made eye contact, then he swiftly disappeared around the building.

Deciding it was time to get a closer look, Hannah stabbed the cigarette into the ashtray, pulled her jacket hood up, and stepped out of the car. She walked up the sidewalk on the even side of the street. An abandoned tricycle missing a back wheel lay on the grass in the parkway strip. She stopped in front of the house directly across the street from Craig's, then knelt and began to tie her Converse All-Stars. She looked up and over while doing it. A lamp was on in the living room, but Hannah couldn't see anyone inside the house.

She got up and continued down the block, counting each house, then crossed the street and continued until she reached the alley. She peered down it. An American Shorthair was perched on the lid of a green metal dumpster. The cat stared at her for a moment then it jumped off and disappeared down a walkway.

Hannah started down the alley, walking under powerlines, past garages, fences, parked cars, and black City and County of Denver trash cans. Her own shadow was more than she wanted to see.

She subtracted each house, and when the count was at two, she shortened her stride, carefully watching every step forward. When it reached one, she ducked down below the fence line. At zero, she crept across the pavement with her knees tucked into her face and glided like a ghost.

Hannah stopped at the back gate and listened. The only sound came from a dog barking two, maybe three blocks to the east. She rested her forehead against the wooden fence and peered through a slat. She could see a refrigerator, stove, cabinets, and a kitchen table. It was clean and tidy.

Placing her palm on the fence, she meticulously rose, never losing her view through the slat.

Standing tall, she watched for a few moments, but there was still no movement in the house. She reached over the top of the fence and put her fingers on the latch, then lifted it until it was unlocked.

Hannah was seconds away from unhooking the latch when Craig walked into the kitchen, talking on a cordless phone. He stopped and looked out the window into the backyard. She instantly dropped back down into a crouch, placing her palm on the ground for balance. Her pulse raced, legs trembling as she watched through the slat, unsure if he'd seen her.

Motionless, she watched him, attempting to read lips, but through a quarter-inch opening, twenty-five feet across a yard, and through a window into a dimly lit kitchen, it was almost impossible.

Then she felt something over her shoulder, staring down on her. She exhaled and slowly started to turn back into the alley.

"Hey! Hey! What are you doing over there?" a man's voice said.

Blinded by a light, she only could see a silhouette across the alley. In one hand was a flashlight, in the other was a trash bag.

"Could you please get that out of my eyes?" she said, using her left hand as a shield from the light and reaching for her mace with her right.

"What are you doing peeping into that house?"

The man continued to point the flashlight into her eyes. After a long, silent moment, he dropped the bag and took a step forward.

"Answer me! Why are you peeping on this house?"

Hannah racked her brain, trying to think of an excuse. "I was looking for my friend's house. I lost the address, but I'm pretty sure it's on this block."

"Bullshit! I watched you for the last five minutes, and you didn't move. You're casing this place," the man said, taking another step forward.

He was now within ten feet of her, and she still couldn't see if he was twenty-five or fifty-five, but by the sound of his voice, she speculated he was older. She didn't want to use her mace, but without knowing if she could outrun him, she didn't have a choice. Slowly, she pulled it out of her pocket.

"What the fuck is going on back there?" Craig yelled from his patio.

"I'm your neighbor, Greg from across the alley. There's some girl out here looking into your house, and I think she might be trying to rob it! I'll watch her if you want to call the cops," the man said, standing on his tippy toes, attempting to see over the fence.

Knowing this could be her only opportunity to flee, Hannah darted up the alley, sprinting faster than she ever had before, disappearing into the night.

She continued for minutes, zigzagging down streets and alleys and across a park before finally succumbing to the side stitches and dropping to her knees behind a Volkswagen Jetta in the parking lot of an Italian restaurant.

At some point in the run, she'd bit down onto her lip, and it was bleeding. Tasting iron, she spit onto the pavement.

Her head was spinning, and it felt like she was going to pass out. She placed her left index and middle finger onto her right wrist and closed her eyes. *One one thousand, two one thousand, three one thousand. Breathe, breathe, breathe.* She continued to reassure herself that she was going to be fine, over and over for the next few minutes until she had the strength to get to her feet.

Tom sat at the kitchen table in the dark, with only a tiny sliver of light beaming across the floor from a living room lamp. His gun lay in the center of the table, casting an inconsequential shadow. He rested his elbows on the table and stared at it for a long time.

After about ten minutes he slid the chair back and started down the hall to the bathroom, where he turned the faucet on hot and wetted a washcloth to wipe his face. Seeing his reflection in the mirror, he couldn't remember the last time he'd consciously looked at himself. The figure was barely recognizable. He'd aged five, maybe ten years—receding hairline, gray hairs, wrinkles under his eyes, dull skin.

Tom returned to the kitchen and walked straight to the liquor cabinet. He poured two shots of Jack Daniel's and swallowed them in one gulp. Then he poured two more and sat at the kitchen table.

Maybe Lisa was right—maybe he needed to leave this town, and maybe burn this house and the ghastly memories to the ground before he left. He thought about where he'd go. Maine? Alaska? The remoteness and solitude could do him some good. He continued sipping on the whiskey and eventually rested his head on his forearms and closed his eyes.

Sometime later, something woke him, a noise from the backyard. Probably an animal, maybe a deer, or a moose—possibly a bear. He inhaled and listened. Seconds later, footsteps crunched into the fresh powder on the patio.

Tom grabbed the gun, slithered out of the chair, then slinked to the back door. He placed his ear against the wall. Dead quiet. Sliding up the wood paneling, he pulled the curtain slightly open. There was a shadow cast onto the snow. He pulled the gun tight against his outer thigh.

As Tom reached for the doorknob, a light tap came at the door, then another a second later.

"Mr. Floyd? Are you home?"

Tom took a step back, "Who the hell is there?"

"It's Katie. We met like two months ago in the Walmart parking lot."

He slid the curtain open and studied the girl. Looking into her eyes, he recalled their brief encounter.

"What the hell are you doing here?"

"I need to talk."

"And you didn't think about calling?"

She looked up at him and shook her head.

"Are you alone?" Tom said.

"Yes, I swear."

Finally, Tom opened the door, and Katie glanced down at the gun before nervously looking back up. Sensing her trepidation, Tom put the weapon in his belt and invited her inside. For a moment, she hesitated. Then she started into the kitchen. Once inside, Tom stopped her and proceeded to give her a thorough pat-down. After he was confident she didn't have any weapons, he invited her to sit at the table.

"And what the fuck are you doing sneaking around my porch in the middle of the night? You were about five seconds from getting shot."

"I saw the kitchen lights were on and thought you might be awake," she said, trailing off.

"And you thought you'd just come on in for a late-night chat?"

"I'm sorry, but I've finally found the strength to talk," she said.

Tom looked at the wall clock, watching each increment of the second hand slowly tick away. He started tapping his fingers in a sequential, rhythmic pattern on the table. Pinky, ring, middle, index. Pinky, ring, middle, index.

That day in the parking lot, he knew she was holding back, not telling everything she knew, and now maybe he'd get genuine answers.

"Do you mind?" Katie said, pulling a pack of Marlboro Reds and packing it against her palm.

"I'd rather you not."

"That wasn't really a question, it was more of a courteous offer that you were supposed to accept since I'm about to tell you things that potentially could get me killed."

"Here," Tom said, sliding an empty glass across the table.

Katie lit a cigarette and inhaled it as if the nicotine provided strength. Tom studied her, still unsure if he could trust her.

"I know I probably come across as some crazy druggie whore, and that's fine, I get it. Hell, up until six months ago, it would've been an accurate assumption of me, but I promise you, everything I tell you tonight is the honest-to-god truth."

Pinky, ring, middle, index, Tom continued on the table.

"And here, this might prove that I'm not full of shit," Katie said.

She opened her purse and started rummaging through the contents, finally removing a five-by-nine picture and sliding it across the table. Tom stopped the picture with his palm and glanced at the glossy image. It was Megan with her arm around Katie.

Tom stared at it for a long time, never blinking. This was the first new picture of Megan he'd seen since she disappeared. Seeing that picture felt like she was almost alive.

Finally, Tom said, "So, why talk now?"

"I owe it to Megan," Katie said, gazing into the glowing cherry of the cigarette. "I'm fucking terrified about what could happen by talking to you, but I know I'm one of the few people still alive who could bring her justice."

"And what do you think could happen to you?"

Katie smirked. "If I'm lucky, a bullet into the back of my head while I'm sleeping." She paused. "Have you heard the name Nathan Cook?"

Tom slowly shook his head.

Sitting at a desk, in a small, windowless office Hannah picked up the previous Sunday's *Rocky Mountain News* and started skimming through the pages. Finally stopping at a story in the local section: "Human Remains Found Near Five Points Confirmed to Be Missing Aurora Mother, Husband Charged."

"Reason twenty-four why I'm still single," she whispered.

Unsure why she opened the paper, she quickly rolled it up and dropped it into the trash can. She opened the

MEGAN FLOYD binder and began flipping the pages, searching for something that she'd missed or overlooked.

About forty minutes later, she heard Marshall walk down the hall, then slam his office door. She checked her watch—it was 11:27.

Hannah got up and walked across the hall and lightly knocked on Marshall's door. As she was about to knock again, the door opened. Marshall greeted her, and they took a seat back at his desk.

"You're never here this late," he said.

"Me? I'm pretty sure I've never seen you in here past seven."

Hannah sat with her legs crossed on the chair, and began studying Marshall's demeanor.

"When was the last time you slept?"

"You know I don't sleep."

"Fine. When was the last time you closed your eyes and tried to sleep?"

Marshall thought for a moment, then pointed to the couch on the opposite wall. "I took a nap yesterday afternoon, probably at least three hours."

Hannah shook her head with motherly disapproval. "Are you still taking those fucking pills?"

Marshall hesitated, then nodded.

"I thought you said you were going to stop"

"I did stop. Then I started again." He coughed, somewhat violently.

"You have one foot in the grave, and I'm not going to stick around to watch you kill yourself."

"A lecture is about the last thing I need right now," he said.

"Oh, you don't want a lecture? How about this? I'm done after this case. That's it. I'm not going to put myself in a situation where I come in some morning and find you dead from a Zoloft overdose."

"You mean Valium."

"Fuck you! I'll quit right now."

"I don't believe you. You love this job, and more importantly, you love me. I know you'd never quit."

"Call my bluff, Marshall, I dare you," Hannah said, leaning forward. "I promise you I'll clean out my desk and never come back if you keep taking those pills."

Marshall leaned back and cocked his head. "You win."

He opened a desk drawer, took out the prescription bottle, and rolled it across the desk. Hannah grabbed it before Marshall could reconsider. She put the bottle in her lap and covered it with her right hand.

"Enough about me. How'd you make out with that guy Craig?" Marshall said.

Over the next half hour, Hannah told Marshall about the trip to the stereo store, following Craig to his house, the neighbor in the alley, and how she'd vomited onto her shoes after sprinting for almost fifteen minutes.

The conversation continued, and Marshall poured himself a glass of whiskey. He offered a pour to Hannah, but she declined.

"How old is that?" she said, pointing to the coffee maker across the room.

"I don't think it's more than a few days old—definitely not more than a week."

Hannah glared at Marshall, then got up and poured a cup. She dumped in three teaspoons of sugar and stirred it with her pinkie.

Leaning in, Tom said, "Who is Nathan Cook?"

"Nathan likes to refer to himself as the Colorado

version of Pablo Escobar—meth mostly, but he dabbles in any illegal substance, as well as the occasional gun deal. It'd take me hours to tell you half the stuff he's done."

Tom was uncertain of the connection between the two, but thoughts of Megan being around Nathan terrified him.

"Did you ever see him kill anyone?" Tom said.

"Not with my eyes, but I overheard stories about him burying bodies in the mountains."

"Did he ever harm you?"

"Are you joking? I lost count of how many times he beat the living shit out of me. One night he choked me during sex until I blacked out, and when I woke up, he laughed about it."

"And you didn't leave him?"

She paused, then swallowed hard.

"No. I tried for a long time, but I was too weak and too scared, and the addiction was too strong. Anyways, I didn't have anywhere to go. I met him when I was sixteen, and within weeks I was using crystal almost daily. I dropped out; my family and friends disowned me. I didn't have any money. He was all I had for a very long time, and I guess while I was with him, it didn't seem that bad."

"I'm sorry. No one should have to go through that, especially a kid."

"It's okay. I'm still here, right?" she said with an empty smile.

At a loss for words, Tom nodded gravely, avoiding eye contact.

"Can we talk about Megan?" she said, redirecting the conversation.

"Yes, sorry," he said. "Did she know Nathan?"

"That's how I met her. She showed up to one of his parties and we ended up getting high all night."

"Do you know how they met?"

"I don't, but if I had to guess, she was buying from him and he was trying to bang her."

"Meth?"

Katie nodded.

Tom ran his fingers through his hair and began cursing under his breath. He felt sick to his stomach.

"Don't feel bad, she hid it very well. Half the time I couldn't even tell when she was high."

"And you guys became close?"

"After that first night, we were pretty much inseparable. I considered her one of my best friends, and still do. I told her secrets I've never told anyone, and she knew more about me than anyone in this fucking world. She was like a sister. I saw her almost every day for months—then she was suddenly gone."

"Tell me about the last time you saw her," Tom said.

"It was that Thursday, sometime after eleven at Nathan's house. I was just watching TV, and she sat down and we talked, drank some beers, and did some lines; neither of us really wanted to get high, but we did it anyways. For the next few hours, I pretty much zoned out on the TV while she played an endless stream of solitaire. Then around three, I got this raging headache, so I told her goodnight and went upstairs, put on my headphones, and crawled into bed."

Tom hung on every word, like he was reading the final chapter of a suspense novel.

"Did you see her after that?"

"No. I got out of bed around six that next morning and nobody was there."

"Was Nathan there that night?" Tom said.

"He was, but he really didn't hang out with us. I think he was doing deals out of the kitchen, but I'm not sure.

"Anyone else?"

"There were always people showing up at that house. I couldn't tell you how many people I'd seen there over the years. But I don't think anyone came over that night. It was strange."

"So, she would've been alone with him?"

"Definitely."

"Was her car there that next morning?"

"Nope. I assumed she'd gone home."

Tom paused momentarily, trying to process everything Katie had just told him.

"When did you suspect something was wrong?"

"The following night, we were going to see Weezer in Denver. She was supposed to pick me up, but she never showed. I knew she'd never ditch me, and that's when I got scared. I asked Nathan, and he told me she'd left around four that morning and he hadn't seen or talked to her since. That night I kept asking him questions and he became more and more unhinged."

Katie cleared her throat and took a sip of water.

"Probably three days later, I saw her picture on the news and knew he was responsible."

"How was he after that?"

"Worse than ever. He was using more, sleeping less, and he became very paranoid. Every little noise he heard outside, he'd grab his gun and rush to the window. About two weeks after she went missing, I got up the nerve and confronted him about what happened that night. He was quiet for what felt like minutes then said, 'I don't know, but I hope it doesn't happen to you.' Then he slowly formed this smile that gave me chills down my entire body. It was the scariest moment of my life—I honestly thought he was going to kill me that night."

"What do you think happened?"

"I've thought about that question so many times, and I honestly don't know. She could've said something he didn't like, or he could've thought she was stealing from him, or he could've found out we were thinking about leaving the state. Honestly, it could've been anything."

"And you think he killed her?"

"I have no doubt," Katie said without hesitation.

The room became silent, and Tom let out a long sigh. As much as he'd prepared himself for this exact moment, it still felt like a Mike Tyson punch to the stomach.

"Why didn't you come forward back then? You could've left an anonymous tip. It would've given us a lead, a new direction."

"I was hoping she'd be found and someone would connect her disappearance to Nathan, but that never happened, and that's when I knew I was in trouble. I was one of the last people to see them together—I could put Megan in Nathan's house the night she disappeared. And I knew he wouldn't hesitate to kill me if he had any inkling that I was going to go to the police. If he did, I'd be buried right next to her."

"Will you give an official statement now?"

"I can't. I haven't seen Nathan in over a year, and I'm safe because I'm not on his radar, but if I talked, he'd find out, and he would not rest until I was dead. I can assure you of that."

"I can promise you protection."

"That's cute, and I think you think that you can, but you can't. You're a cop and you couldn't protect Megan, so how the fuck do you think you are going to protect me?" She lit a cigarette. "After I walk out that door, I'm getting in my car and heading east on I-70 and never coming back."

Tom started to speak, but Katie stopped him.

"I need to run, so this is the last thing I can help with," she said, pulling a piece of paper out of her pocket. "That's the address to the house. His dad owns it, but he didn't live there when I was staying there. I can't remember the exact reason, but I think he was working or living with a girlfriend on the East Coast, or something. I heard he moved back and Nathan moved out. The house is on like ten acres, it's huge." Katie paused for a moment. "I have a feeling you'll find her body somewhere on that property."

Tom stared at the paper for a moment. "How can I reach you again?"

"You won't. I can almost promise that unless I end up in the morgue, this will be the last time you'll see me."

"At least take my number."

She shook her head. Tom jumped out of the chair and grabbed a notepad hanging from the refrigerator. He scribbled down his number, tore off the top sheet, and held it out to Katie. She stared at the paper for a few seconds before turning to the door.

Tom grabbed her hand. "Please just take it."

Katie looked at him long and steadily, then slipped it into her front pocket. With her hand on the doorknob, she glanced back to Tom.

"Before she went to work on that last day, we met up in Silverthorne and were talking about leaving Colorado and starting over in some town in Florida where nobody knew who we were. A fresh start, you know? Every day, I wish we would've gotten in her car and left this place forever."

Before Tom could respond, she disappeared out the door, closing it softly behind her.

Katie started the engine, turned the heat on high, and began rubbing her hands in front of the vent. The air was cold, almost colder than it was outside the car. She continued rubbing until the air turned from frigid to slightly warm. After a couple minutes, she latched the seatbelt, put the car into drive, and turned east onto County Road 50.

She glanced into the rearview mirror, then quickly looked away.

"I should've known you were following me," Katie muttered.

"I wouldn't be here if you'd stayed away."

Nathan rested the barrel of a Beretta M9 on the center console and tilted his head up.

"Now don't do anything stupid or else I'll have to mess up that pretty little face."

Katie leaned back and firmly grabbed the steering wheel. Briefly, she contemplated stepping on the gas and turning full speed into a tree. She knew her odds for survival would be low, but Nathan wasn't wearing a seatbelt, so he would most likely die in a high-speed head-on collision.

"You shouldn't have been at his house, Katie."

"I didn't tell him anything about you, I promise," she said.

"Shh, I know you're lying, and I don't want to hear any of your lies right now."

Nathan sat up and shifted into the seat behind her. He began petting her hair, then leaned forward and brought a handful of it into his face. He closed his eyes and inhaled the scent.

"I've missed you Katie. I really have. Have you missed me?"

SIX

T om eased the 4Runner to a stop on the long dirt road. About a quarter mile up the driveway was a single-story house with an old beat-up Ford pickup truck parked in front. He reached for the map in the passenger seat and opened it, placing it on top of the steering wheel. This was the address Katie gave him, he was sure of it.

Tom called the house numerous times, but the phone just rang. No answer, no machine, just indefinite ringing. He suspected he'd arrive at the house and it would be abandoned, but a steady stream of smoke billowed out of the chimney. Someone was living there, and he was going to find out who.

Larry lay back in the leather recliner with the leg rest up, drifting in and out of sleep. The TV was on CNN, but muted. His eyes were heavy when he heard a car engine.

Slamming down the leg rest, he sat up and listened. After a few moments, he trudged to the front window.

Carefully opening the curtain, he peeked out, watching a 4Runner slowly drive up the driveway. He didn't recognize the vehicle and didn't know anyone who drove a Toyota, or for that matter any foreign-made car.

He walked to the closet, grabbed his shotgun, and returned to the front door. With one eye closed, he squinted through the peephole, waiting for the 4Runner to get into view.

Tom slowly drove up the driveway and parked about a hundred feet from the porch. After surveying the house, he put the car in gear and opened the glove box. Grabbing his gun, he secured it on his hip holster. He took a deep breath, opened the door, and set his boots onto the gravel.

The sun was shining through the clouds, birds were chirping and there was a slight breeze. Looking up Tom watched a plane for a few seconds until it disappeared into the clouds.

He had an uneasy feeling in his stomach. It reminded him of the only time he'd been shot at—a domestic dispute call that should've been routine, but as he walked up the sidewalk, the front door swung open and the boyfriend fired three shots, one coming inches from his temple. Tom fell to the ground and fired two shots at the boyfriend. One of them hitting the man in the chest, killing him instantly. That was the second worse day of Tom's life.

After a silent prayer he started to the house.

Larry watched the man walk toward the front door. He'd never seen him before, and no stranger should set foot on his property for any reason unannounced. He couldn't remember the last time someone besides Nathan had been there, but at best guess, it'd been at least a year or two.

Maybe this guy was looking for Nathan, attempting to settle an old debt, or maybe Nathan had sent the man to execute him in hopes of inheriting the property. Larry smiled. The joke was on Nathan, because Larry had updated his will years ago, giving the house, the property, and everything on it to his sister in Idaho. He'd left Nathan nothing.

Larry looked down at the gun, then through the peephole. The man was about forty feet away. After leaving the Army, Larry had made a promise to himself that he'd never point the muzzle of a gun at another man again. He exhaled. Some promises are unattainable, no matter how hard they should be kept.

At about twenty feet, Larry unlocked the deadbolt, secured the rifle, and placed his hand on the doorknob. He stepped to the right, then slowly started to turn the knob.

Tom was about ten feet away from the porch when the front door swung open. A man was standing in the doorway, pointing the barrel of a shotgun directly at him. Tom instantly recognized the face from an old mugshot he'd discovered during his investigation into the property. The eyes were aged, the beard was gray, and he was about twenty pounds heavier, but it was unquestionably Larry, Nathan's father.

Frozen, Tom felt his heart pound against his chest. He

started searching for any place to take cover, but there was nothing— he was a sitting duck.

"You got about five seconds to tell me what the fuck you're doing here," Larry said, stepping out onto the porch.

"My name is Tom Floyd. I used to be a deputy up in Grand County."

"I don't give a fuck who you are or what you did. You're on my property, and I don't take kindly to strangers, so you better tell me what the fuck you're doing up here before I blow your goddamn head off."

Larry stepped forward, never taking aim off Tom.

"I'm here because of my daughter. She went missing about two years ago." Tom paused, catching his breath. "Her name was Megan Floyd, and I believe your son killed her."

Larry stood there motionless. His pupils dilated, leaving a small sliver of white around his eyes. Finally, he lowered the rifle to his side until the muzzle met the porch.

"Come on inside," he said.

They sat at the kitchen table, each with a Miller High Life in front of them. Larry looked down at the can, picked it up, and tilted his head back, then took a long drink. He placed the can onto the table, moving it in a small, counterclockwise circle.

"You really think Nathan had something to do with your daughter's disappearance? Megan, was it?"

"Yes. I'm positive he was involved, and I suspect he killed her in this house and buried her somewhere on this property."

Larry leaned back into the chair, removed the black handkerchief from his pants pocket, and blew his nose.

"I always knew someone would come knocking on my door about something like this. I prayed it'd never happen,

THE FEAR OF WINTER

but deep down in my gut, I knew it would. I'm just glad his mother isn't around to see it," Larry said, staring into the bottom of the beer can.

He paused for a second, cracking the knuckles on each hand. "I truly believe he was born with the devil inside him. Just like some kids are born to be great athletes or musicians, Nathan was destined to become what he is now."

"And what is that?" Tom said.

"A monster, through and through."

Katie peered down at her ankles. The skin was raw, with crusted blood on her flesh and the metal restraints. The cuffs were locked tightly, only about a quarter of an inch between the metal and her ankles. They were attached to a three-foot rusted chain that was locked to a heavy-duty D-Ring bolted to the cement floor.

The small, dark, damp cellar was about ten feet by ten feet, cement floor to ceiling. The only source of light was a single light bulb with a pull chain. The wall to her right had large water stains at the top that she suspected were due to a leaky toilet or sink. On the opposite side, the cellar door opened to a rickety staircase that led into the backyard. When fully stretched, Katie could almost touch the door, but it didn't matter because it had two deadbolts that were keyed on both sides.

She sat on top of two stained comforters that lay on a large dog bed. An arm's length to her right stood a five-gallon bucket that she was using as a crude toilet. Two milk crates and a piece of plywood formed a table that had three books: *Blood Meridian* by Cormac McCarthy, *Fear and Loathing in Las Vegas* by Hunter Thompson, and

Fahrenheit 451 by Ray Bradbury, as well as a small Sony CD player next to a stack of about twenty discs, mostly classic rock and alternative.

She'd yelled the first night, but after about ten minutes, Nathan opened the door holding a steak knife. He told her if she continued screaming, he'd cut her tongue out.

While reading the final chapter of *Fear and Loathing* she heard footsteps walking down the stairs. She placed the book on the table and stared at the door. The first deadbolt unlocked, then the second one. The door opened, and a sliver of sunlight beamed onto the floor. This was the first time in days she'd seen natural light, and it was blinding for a few moments.

Nathan ducked through the doorway and walked into the room. He held a five-gallon bucket in one hand, and in the other was a grocery bag containing a half sleeve of saltine crackers, some pieces of hard candy, two Granny Smith apples, three twelve-ounce bottles of water, and one roll of toilet paper.

"Does that need to be replaced?" Nathan said, pointing to the bucket.

Katie nodded.

Nathan switched out the buckets and placed the used one in the doorway. He turned back to Katie.

"How are you doing, my love?"

She looked up to him. "Could you please take these off my ankles? I'm losing feeling in my toes," Katie said, pointing to the restraints.

"You know I can't do that."

"Please. I promise I won't try anything."

"If you are good for the next few days, I'll think about loosening them."

Tears began running down her cheeks and dripping

onto her shirt. All she wanted was to wrap the chain around his neck until life escaped him.

"I'm trying to play nice with you, but you have to play nice with me. And if you do what I say, I might let you out, but if you don't, I'll make your stay very unpleasant," Nathan said.

"I'll do anything you want if you let me out. I'm starting to go crazy sitting down here."

"I already know that, and I don't have to let you out of the room to make you do what I want. You've made mistakes, and unfortunately, I have to teach you a lesson, so please don't make those mistakes again. Do you understand?"

"Yeah," Katie said, barely audible.

"I didn't hear you."

"Yes, I understand."

Nathan smiled. "I've missed you being around. You really have a way to brighten up a room."

"I've missed you too. I should have never left; it was so dumb of me. I've always known in my heart that we belong together," Katie said.

That was a lie. Katie wanted to say she detested him. He was a coward that got pleasure out of torturing women half his size, but she knew if she questioned his masculinity, he'd probably leave her dead body in the forest for the coyotes.

Nathan stepped over the table and knelt in front of Katie. Calmly, he placed his palm on the back of her head and pulled her head forward until it was inches from his. They stared into each other's eyes. Katie wanted to look away, but she didn't. Then he leaned in and kissed her forehead.

"I need you to make a phone call for me."

Katie nodded dejectedly.

He handed her a piece of paper. She read it, then looked back up to Nathan.

"Don't look at me, look at the paper. Look at the fucking paper!"

Katie diverted her eyes back down, studying it for the next few minutes. Nathan continued to hover over her, almost like a statue. She felt his gaze on her and knew he'd hurt her if she made a single mistake.

After a long silence, Nathan said, "Are you ready?"

"Yes," she said, nodding again.

"Remember, just say what is written down, and everything should be fine."

Nathan pressed talk on the cordless phone, dialed, and handed the phone to Katie.

"Hello, is this Marshall York?" Katie said, glancing up at Nathan.

He nodded and smiled.

Tom sat across the kitchen table from Larry, telling him how he believed Nathan had abducted and killed Megan. Telling another man that his child was a murderer was not something anyone should have to do. After Tom finished, Larry remained silent for a long time.

Finally, he said, "I came home early from work one day and Nathan's car was in the driveway, but I couldn't find him anywhere. Then I go in the backyard and see this little plume of smoke coming from the forest. I start walking in the direction of the smoke, and about ten minutes later I start to hear the crackling of the fire, then see the flames through the opening of the trees. At first, I could only see the fire, but then I saw this Black Lab lying in front of the flames. It was just lying there, not moving. Then I saw the wood of a knife handle sticking out of its fucking neck. Finally, I saw Nathan, on his knees, behind the dog. He was staring into the fire, in some trancelike state. He starts making this low-pitched, constant humming noise, almost like some incoherent chant, then rips the knife out and starts slashing his forearm, letting the blood drip onto the dog. It was something you'd see in a goddamn horror movie."

Tom could hear the pain in Larry's voice, the shame, the guilt. Nathan had destroyed what was once a good man.

"I mean, I saw some fucked-up shit overseas while I was in the Army, but seeing my nineteen-year-old kid in front of that fire has given me nightmares. It's one of the moments that you try and forget, but it's one that stays with you forever. And if that wasn't my kid, I would've walked back to the house and grabbed my shotgun and put some buckshot through him and shoved his body into the fire like a piece of trash, but he is my blood, my only child. What the hell was I supposed to do?"

"I don't know. I don't. No one should have to see something like that," Tom said.

Larry swallowed hard. "I knew he was beyond help and decided to run. I took a job in upstate New York a month later, left him the keys to the house, and didn't come back for almost four years. Those last few nights, I truly thought he was going to sneak into my room when I was sleeping and bring the backend of a claw hammer into my skull." The man straightened his trucker cap. "I miss Nancy more than anything, but I'm thankful she passed when she did because it would've destroyed her to see what Nathan has become. She was a damn strong woman, but she couldn't have saved him either."

"It's not too late to fix this. Help me find him so he

doesn't hurt anyone again," Tom said, leaning into the table.

Larry looked up at him, then shied away.

"He killed Megan," Tom persisted, "and probably others, and I promise you he'll do it again. He will not stop until he is caught."

"I'm afraid I'll be very little help. I haven't seen him in weeks, and before that it was probably a year."

"Wait, you've seen him in the last few weeks?"

Larry turned back to a calendar hanging on the refrigerator between two old Denver Broncos schedule magnets.

"If I remember right, it was Sunday the seventh. He just showed up out of the blue at the butt crack of dawn, probably around six, six thirty. I watched his truck pull up and waited for him to come inside, but he never did, so I got up to see what he was doing. Turns out he was searching for something in the shed."

"Do you know what he was looking for?"

"I don't know. When I opened the back door, he closed the shed, zipped up his backpack, and started walking back to his truck. I yelled and asked what he was doing, and he just looks up at me and smiles—then continues walking without saying a word. I haven't seen him since."

Larry speculated that Nathan had hidden drugs, guns, or something illegal and came on an early Sunday morning to retrieve them, in hopes Larry would still be sleeping, or passed out.

"Do you mind if I go take a look?" Tom said.

"Sure, be my guest."

They walked out to the shed together, and after Larry unlocked the padlock, Tom began the search. There was a gas-powered mower, four shovels of various sizes, a plastic rake with some missing tines, random tools, a ceramic planter, stacked bags of soil, and lawn chairs that were at least a decade old. After about five minutes, Tom knew that whatever Nathan came for, he took, and there wasn't going to be anything inside that shed that could connect him to Megan.

They walked back to the house, where Larry opened two more beers, handing one to Tom. They drank for a long while without saying anything.

"I'm so sorry about your daughter."

Tom nodded and ran his hand through his beard.

"You know, for the first time since Megan went missing—we're going on over two years—I feel like I'm close, really close. And Nathan is the key to solving her disappearance," Tom said.

"I could've stopped him," Larry muttered.

"I don't think you could've ever known he'd turn into what he has become."

"Yes, I did. That day in the forest, I saw with my own two eyes that he's a monster. I should've ended him right there. Nobody would've ever known, and within weeks, nobody would've cared."

Tom started to respond, but he stopped. He knew he couldn't say it, but he wanted to tell Larry he should've ended that bastard's life that very day. The world would've been better off without Nathan on it, and they both knew it.

Tom closed his mouth and picked up the beer, placing it against his lips.

"Ever been to the Black Bear Inn, down in Lakewood, off Morrison?" Larry said.

"No, but I've driven by it a bunch of times."

Larry got up and walked over to the kitchen counter, opened a drawer, and picked out a matchbook, which he tossed onto the table. Tom stared at the matchbook with a logo from the Black Bear Inn for a few silent moments.

"I'm sure it's a long shot, but this has to be his. It ain't mine, so it must've fallen out of Nathan's car, or pocket or something. I'm guessing this is one of his hangouts." Larry paused for a moment and cracked his neck.

"Do you still have any pictures of him?" Tom said.

Without acknowledging the question, Larry turned and vanished down the hallway. He returned, holding a single photo.

"This is probably five or six years old, but he pretty much looks exactly the same."

Tom studied the picture for what felt like forever. It was the first time he'd seen the face of the man who killed Megan, and every feature was instantaneously burned into his memory.

After a long silence, Larry said, "That's all I got—I'm sorry I couldn't be more help."

"No, this gives me something. Thank you."

Tom stood up and extended his arm for a handshake. Larry gripped it.

"If Nathan really is responsible for your daughter, I'd be very careful when you find him."

"I will."

"And one more thing," Larry said, still grasping Tom's hand.

"What's that?"

"If you find him, don't hesitate with what I should've done that day in the forest."

Larry watched Tom walk to his 4Runner, then watched as the vehicle drove up the driveway. Motionless, he waited until the dust cloud disappeared. Then he returned to the kitchen. He grabbed a bottle of Jim Beam and began chugging from it. After six large gulps, he set the bottle back down and rested his hands on the counter.

Outside the kitchen window, he stared into the luminous mountain skyline. The wind howled against the glass pane. He stood there for a long time and watched the dusk turn into darkness.

After the sun vanished, he picked up the bottle and walked into the living room, taking three more pulls. He sat in the recliner, pulled out his wallet, and removed a faded picture of Nancy. It was taken in 1975, during their first vacation, a road trip across the west to California. Nancy was on Mission Beach, wearing a polka-dot two-piece swimsuit. Feet in the sand, back to the ocean, and the sun setting overhead. This was how he wanted to remember her.

He kissed the picture, placed it on his chest, and closed his eyes. Then he reached for the .357 Magnum on the end table and positioned the muzzle under the soft part of his chin.

"I'm coming home, babe," Larry said.

Then he pulled the trigger.

Hannah ordered a large latte with a shot of milk, then walked to a corner table in the café and sat down. She looked down at her watch just as it flipped to 7:34. She couldn't remember the last time she was out in public this early, let alone awake.

Sipping on her coffee, she watched people on the sidewalk outside the café. She pitied the nine-to-fivers, rushing to work not to be late so a boss they hated wouldn't yell at them, just to pay the mortgage for a house out in the suburbs, in a loveless marriage probably only still intact because divorce would be traumatizing to the children.

Over the years, she'd worked countless cases of unfaithful husbands. They all had the same story—they loved their wives and children, but they were bored with life and began fucking a co-worker, or the girl at the gym, or the Chili's waitress. Those women provided the excitement they needed in their lives. Once caught, they all swore it was a moment of weakness, that they'd never be unfaithful again. Most of them would reconcile with their wives, but the damage was done, life slowly circling the drain.

"Hannah?" Ethan said.

She turned around and smiled. Ethan was wearing a black suit with a gray tie and black Allen Edmonds Oxford shoes, holding a leather briefcase that looked expensive. He was a decade older than her, but didn't look it. She'd hoped that he'd have put on twenty pounds or developed male pattern baldness, but he looked better than the last time she'd seen him.

"What has it been? A year, year and a half?" Ethan said.

"Almost two."

She remembered the exact date. It was her birthday, and the last time they'd slept together—the last time she'd slept with anyone.

"That long, huh? I guess you're probably right. You were always better at that type of stuff." He took a sip of coffee. "Well, you still look amazing as ever."

She thanked him and returned the compliment. They spent the next few minutes catching up.

"Stacy and I got engaged. We're getting married this summer up in Vail."

"Congratulations! I'm so, so happy for you guys," Hannah said, her stomach turning.

At one point, Hannah had thought their relationship would evolve into something more, but after three months, she discovered she was the other woman, a side piece of the sort Ethan had probably had numerous times before and since.

She despised herself for getting involved with him; she despised herself for being naïve. As pathetic as it sounded, she still loved him. She missed his breath in her ears, his lips on her neck, and his arms wrapped around her body. His touch, his smell. Everything.

They chatted for twenty more minutes, all of which was insignificant, but it made her feel special again.

After glancing down at his watch, Ethan said, "So, I found what you wanted, but remember, I'm only doing this because, well, I owe you, so this is a one-time-only request."

"I know, I know. I promise I won't ever ask you for anything again."

Ethan opened his briefcase, removed a manila folder, and opened it.

"The owner of the house at 3943 Navajo is Craig William Turner, born July 6, 1964, Denver, Colorado. He purchased the house for $96,000 in 1993 and has never missed a mortgage payment."

"Yes, I already know all of that. Do you have something I don't know?" Hannah said.

Ethan stared at her for a moment. "This took a little digging, but he purchased a property outside of Aspen Park back in the summer of '95. It was through an LLC called TWC Inc."

"His initials backwards," Hannah whispered.

"And it's TWC's only asset. I did more searching but I couldn't find much—no physical address, just a PO Box out of north Denver."

"What do you know about that property?"

"It's a little over seven acres, and from what I can find the only dwelling is an old, decrepit barn built in the seventies. The closest neighbor is like half a mile."

"This is up by Lone Peak," Hannah said, reading the documents.

Ethan nodded. "What's this about?"

"A missing girl," Hannah said without looking up. That was more than she wanted to tell him.

"And this barn is connected to her?"

"Maybe, I don't know."

"Let me guess—you're going to break in and search it by yourself."

Hannah nodded.

"Fuck, Hannah, please be careful."

"I'm a big girl. You don't have to worry about me."

She looked up and smiled, and Ethan smiled back. An awkward silence followed.

"Can I have this?" Hannah said, pointing to the paper.

"It's all yours."

"Thanks. I gotta run," she said, slipping the paper into her purse.

"Maybe we could go grab a drink sometime and catch up," Ethan said.

She looked down at him. He wasn't her best, but he was always fun, and she deeply missed him. For a moment, she contemplated forgetting the world, getting a hotel room and fucking all day, but she knew she'd despise herself before sunrise.

"I don't think that's a good idea."

"Why not?"

"We both know what would happen after said drinks."

Ethan smiled.

"See you around," she said.

"Take care of yourself, Hannah."

"Always." She paused. "Tell Stacy I said hi."

A single spotlight above the entrance of the Black Bear Inn shone down onto the dirt parking lot. There were seven cars scattered there, and it'd been almost an hour since anyone entered or exited the bar.

Tom leaned back into the driver's seat and watched the moon vanish behind a billow of thick, milky clouds. It reappeared a few moments later, brighter than before.

After taking a sip of coffee, he rolled down the window six inches and listened to the night. A loud banging metal sound came from the distance, maybe trash cans knocked over by the wind or someone slamming the lid of a dumpster. It came and went as the wind whistled through the tiny opening.

It was just after ten. He'd been in the parking lot for almost three hours, making a grand total of thirteen hours over the last four nights. He planned to be parked in the same location every night until Nathan was found or Megan's case was solved.

Half an hour later, a beat-up Ford F150 pulled in and parked two spots left of the entrance. Tom hastily leaned forward, resting his chin on the steering wheel. He watched, motionless.

The truck idled, headlights shining onto the building, taillights beaming into the dirt. Tom could see the silhouette of a man and woman. Finally, the lights turned off, the doors opened, and the couple started walking to the entrance.

The woman stopped and looked back at Tom, making eye contact. They stared at each other for a second, then she said something to the man. Without looking back, the man grabbed her arm and pulled her to the door.

As they walked into the bar, the sound of the jukebox playing "Wichita Lineman" by Glen Campbell echoed across the parking lot. As the door shut, the music quickly faded.

Hannah turned onto North Turkey Creek Road off Highway 285. She slowed at a fork in the road, then flipped on the blinker and turned right onto High Drive. Slowing to a stop, she looked down at the highlighted address on the paper and continued up the road.

Almost six miles up High Drive, the pavement turned to gravel, and shortly after that, she was traversing over washboards up the twisting road. The snow drifts on either side of the road were two or three feet high—they probably wouldn't fully melt until mid-May.

There was an occasional house or driveway to a house hidden by the forest, and the only sign of life was the rare porch light and smoke billowing from chimneys.

She stopped the car and rolled down the window. A gust of wind hit her in the face through the small opening. It was crisp. She looked around. Even though she was less than an hour west of Denver and civilization, the forest felt endless and forbidding.

Continuing up the road, she spotted a barn in a clearing about two hundred feet off to the side. Hannah stopped, turned off the headlights, and grabbed the binoculars from the passenger seat. She watched the barn for a long time.

Thoughts of a hike outside Georgetown the previous summer infiltrated her head. About a mile into the hike, an enormous evergreen had fallen about fifteen feet in front of her on the trail. It shook the earth. Give or take a couple seconds, and she would have been in the path of the tree. If she hadn't stopped to tie her shoe minutes earlier, she could've been crushed along with everything else it annihilated. An inconsequential, everyday event saved her life. Thinking about how fragile life could be kept her up at night.

Hannah dropped the binoculars, then continued driving on the road. About a quarter of a mile farther, there was a small trailhead parking lot utilized by hikers. The lot was empty. She parked and turned off the car. Then she opened the glove box and removed her Beretta, a flashlight, and a pair of winter gloves. Stepping out, she started walking up the road in the direction of the barn. It was only 4:32, but the sun was already fading behind the mountain peaks to the west. The entire forest would be completely dark within twenty minutes.

Jogging up the road, it took about ten minutes to reach the turnout. She removed the flashlight and shined it onto the snow between the road and the barn. The snow was undisturbed, with no tracks from man or animal.

She started toward the barn, post-holing each step up to her knees. The air was harsh on her lungs, and she was having difficulty catching her breath. She tripped about halfway, partly from the snow and partly from exhaustion. Picking herself up, Hannah brushed off her jacket and removed the snow out of her gloves.

A shiver ran through her. All she wanted was her Discman with Radiohead playing on repeat. Music always eased her nerves.

She arrived at the barn about thirty minutes after leaving the car. Crouching against the decaying structure, she wiped sweat out of her eyes and off her forehead. The forest was silent except for her own breathing.

After about a minute, she stood up and turned on the flashlight, but then clicked it off almost instantly. A pickup truck engine broke the silence, echoing through the forest. She leaned into the barn and watched the road, then saw headlights coming toward the bend. Remaining very still, she watched the road anxiously.

The truck slowed as it approached the bend, and Hannah thought for a second it had stopped, but it turned the corner and the taillights disappeared into the night. She remained still for another minute, waiting until the forest was silent again.

Suddenly, a feeling that someone was watching consumed her. For a brief moment she thought about walking back to her car, driving home, and climbing under the sheets with Milo.

She watched the road for another few minutes, then clicked the flashlight back on, shining it onto the snow, and walked to the front of the barn, where she moved the light up and down the sliding door. It was nailed shut, with seven two-by-fours running the entire length of the door, spread out at one-foot intervals. Even if she'd brought a crowbar, she didn't have the strength to remove one board, let alone seven.

"Well, somebody doesn't want anyone getting into this fucking barn," she whispered.

Lumbering along the south side of the barn, she moved the light up and down over the weathered wood. There were two windows—well, she assumed they'd been windows at one point, but now they were covered with plywood and nailed shut.

Hannah continued, stepping in snow drifts two to three feet deep. Toward the back of the barn, she spotted a break in the wood. Dropping to her knees she started shoveling snow away with her hands. Minutes later, she reached the dirt and studied the opening. It was about a foot wide and probably a foot and a half high. Sticking her head through, she aimed the flashlight into the barn.

In the middle of the barn floor was a large object covered by a tarp caked with dust, dirt, and probably animal droppings. Pieces of plywood were leaned sporadically against the object, but Hannah could make out the outline of a vehicle. She had a gut feeling it was Megan's Chevy Blazer.

Examining the opening, Hannah estimated there was an inch or two of clearance to squeeze through, but if she was wrong, she'd be trapped, and probably be dead within hours. A rather miserable one at that, slowly freezing to death, trapped in a small hole. It'd be months, maybe years before her body would be discovered.

The wind pierced through her jacket as she watched a thick, milky cloud of breath exit her mouth. Her feet were cold, her toes freezing, and her hands were violently shaking. The temperature was rapidly dropping. She began cursing herself for not wearing proper winter attire.

Hannah picked up a rock and tossed it into the forest. The rock dropped to the earth about five seconds later, and then there was nothing. Just her, and the barn, and her thoughts, and the unknown.

She placed her gun and flashlight inside the barn, closed her eyes, and put both arms through the opening. Turning from side to side, she began squirming across the dirt. About a quarter of the way through, she felt something run across her neck and stopped. She remained still, then realized it was her mind playing tricks.

Shifting onto her back, she brought her arms to her side, then pushed out onto the slats, sliding across the dirt until her knees were through the opening. After her entire body was inside the barn, she sat up and grabbed the flashlight and gun. She remained still for a long time, focusing on her breathing.

Hannah stood up and shined the light onto the tarp—it was definitely an SUV, most likely a Blazer or Bronco.

"Please, please, please," she whispered.

At the front of the vehicle, she bent down, grabbed the tarp, and slowly started to lift it. Hannah froze as soon as she saw the Colorado license plate screwed to the bumper. It was Megan's license plate number.

Taking a step back, she stared at the vehicle, coming in and out of focus. At first, the discovery didn't feel real, and she had to double- and triple-check the license plate. Then, after a long moment, she realized that she had just made the biggest breakthrough of the biggest unsolved Colorado Missing Person case of the last fifty years. Hannah was always even-keeled—this was a rare moment of excitement for her.

Finding the vehicle removed some of her doubt that she was an inept investigator, and gave her confidence that maybe she'd be able to discover the clue that'd eventually lead to her sister's killer. A rare smile formed.

Fifty minutes later, Hannah pulled into the parking lot of the Long Peak Saloon. She was so excited about her discovery that she took a corner a little too fast and almost slid off the road into a ditch. After that near mishap, she obeyed the speed limit.

She parked and grabbed two quarters, then walked across the dirt parking lot to the payphone. A man stumbled out of the bar and down the stairs toward the lot. Hannah turned and watched him. He walked between two trucks, unzipped his pants, and began urinating on the back tire of a Ford F150. He made eye contact and nodded. Hannah nodded back and continued to the phone.

She inserted the coins and dialed. The phone rang four times. Then the answering machine message played.

Hannah patiently waited for the beep. "It's Hannah. I found her car. I fucking found it!" She said, her voice frantic. She paused for a second, attempting to gather her thoughts. "It was her Blazer, her license plate. It was Megan's fucking car!" She paused again, then smiled. "It was pretty much empty minus a couple cigarette butts and soda cans, but I didn't get a chance to do an extensive search. It's in this abandoned barn up by Lone Peak, and it was freezing and pitch dark, so I was thinking we could head back up there tomorrow when we have some sunlight. I'm still up in Indian Hills, so I'll be back at the office in like an hour. Talk to you soon."

Hannah turned back toward her car. The man was gone, but a tiny stream of urine traversed down the parking lot.

Marshall slammed the car door. It echoed throughout the nearly empty parking garage. He glanced down at his watch and saw that it was 2:24. Six minutes early. He tapped the screen then looked to the early nineties Ford Taurus about twenty parking spots to his right.

For a moment, he thought he saw movement inside the vehicle, but then he realized the garage lights were creating shadows that weren't there. He eyed the Taurus for another two minutes.

Clearing his throat, he lit a cigarette and blew the smoke up to the cement ceiling.

He was somewhat reluctant taking a meeting with an unknown caller, in an empty parking garage in downtown Denver, in the middle of the night, in the dead of winter, completely alone. But Marshall always agreed to anonymous meetings with someone who said they had "pertinent" information on a case. In most instances, the informant was a liar or a delusional drug addict, or suffered from some sort of psychiatric disorder, but on the rarest occasions, he'd hit paydirt. Marshall was certain this would be an inconsequential meeting, but if it was, he was only twenty minutes from his house.

"Fuck you motherfucker, that's mine," a voice yelled.

Marshall turned back to the ledge.

"That's my bag. I found it fair and square, so fuck off," another voice yelled.

"Give it to me, it's mine!" the first voice yelled.

"I'll rip out your throat if you don't back away."

Marshall looked over the ledge and down the three stories to Market Street. The street was empty. The voices sounded like they were directly below him, but they were probably around the block.

It was 2:29. He walked to the back of his car, leaned against the trunk, sucked the last remaining drag, then dropped the cigarette, smashing it with the heel of his boot.

A moment later, the sound of an engine roared through the lower levels of the parking garage. Marshall turned to the ramp entrance. The engine got louder, and louder, and louder, and then headlights appeared on the curved cement walls.

The truck stopped at the crest of the ramp, a red-and-green mid-eighties Chevy Suburban. It idled momentarily, then continued at a walking pace before stopping next to the Taurus. Black smoke billowed out of the tailpipe, surrounding the vehicle in a carbon monoxide cloud.

Uneasily, Marshall gave a quick thumbs-up, then motioned to the adjacent parking spot. The engine idled for a moment, then the Suburban continued toward him, this time at a crawl.

"I don't like this," Marshall whispered.

The car was six spots away, then five, then four. It stopped in the middle of the parking lane, engine revving.

Marshall squinted through the headlights until he could make out the license plate, repeating it silently until he was confident it was memorized.

He began cursing himself for not vetting the caller and foolishly agreeing to a location that left him wide open and vulnerable. He was getting sloppy in his old age, or maybe the alcohol or pill addiction was clouding his instincts.

Marshall peered over his shoulder and considered running for the ledge and jumping to the street below. Three stories onto a sidewalk would be a survivable fall, but he wasn't as agile as he had been in his thirties, and he could have a couple bullets in his spine before reaching the ledge. Stand his ground and fight—that was his only option.

The headlights turned off, and the V8 engine roared.

Marshall jumped back, crouched, and leaned into the fender of his truck. The Suburban got louder and louder, and the cement started to tremble.

Reaching back, he removed his gun, extended his arm, and slipped his finger onto the trigger. He took a deep breath and steadied his aim, then fired twice, both bullets hitting the front windshield.

The Suburban turned away from Marshall, skidding to a stop. The muzzle of a gun emerged out the driver's window, and then there were two flashes, followed by two deafening bangs. Marshall fired twice more, both hitting the lower section of the door panel. For a second, the garage was eerily quiet. Then the Suburban sped off and

Marshall fired one last time, missing the truck completely, the bullet ricocheting off the ceiling.

Marshall remained still for a second, then felt the pain and dropped to his knees in a pool of blood. Looking down at his jacket, he found that it was blood-soaked. His vision blurred, and he fell forward onto his palms, then dropped to his elbows. His breathing was labored, and he started sucking for air.

"Help," Marshall said, barely audible. He cried out again, this time a little louder.

Finally, his left arm gave out, and he dropped to the ground, his face landing hard against the blood-soaked concrete. He coughed, then attempted to spit, but his mouth was dry. At that moment all he wanted was water. A single sip.

His breathing began to slow, and his eyes became heavy.

Don't close your eyes, don't fucking close your eyes.

If he did, odds were he'd never open them again. Marshall stared up at the dull, white parking garage lights. They started flickering, then began spinning. He blinked to focus, but his vision was fading.

Breathe, just breathe. You're not going to fucking die right here, not tonight. Somebody heard the shots, and help will be here soon. You just need to hold on for a few more minutes. Breathe.

He wiped the sweat off his forehead and lifted his head a couple of inches, looking across the parking garage. Nothing. Then his head plummeted to the concrete, splashing blood onto his left cheek.

"Please, help," Marshall muttered.

He rolled onto his back and stared at the ceiling, then slowly closed his eyes as the blood began drowning his lungs.

SEVEN

H annah pulled into a parking spot on the second level at Saint Joseph Hospital. Both feet were on the pavement before the car had stopped moving. She started jogging down the ramp, but that quickly turned into a near sprint.

He can't be dead. He can't be.

Hannah dashed into the Emergency Room lobby and went directly to the check-in desk. She tapped her fingers on the counter. The nurse looked up from a computer screen, glasses on the edge of her nose.

"I received a call that Marshall York was transported here. Can you tell me if he's out of surgery?"

The nurse stared at Hannah for a moment, then started typing.

"May I ask your name and relationship to Mr. York?"

"I'm Hannah York, and he's my stepdad," Hannah said without hesitation, knowing they'd only provide information to immediate family. "My mother is a complete mess. I need to know how he's doing so I can give her some sort of reassurance."

The nurse studied Hannah. Then she pushed the glasses to the bridge of her nose and looked down at the computer screen.

"What was the name again?"

"Marshall York," she said louder.

The nurse started typing, moving the mouse and making the occasional click. Hannah leaned in, trying to view the screen.

"I'm going to page Doctor Coleman to come talk to you. Could you please take a seat in the waiting room?" the nurse said.

"Just tell me what room he's in. I need to see him now."

Hannah felt an emptiness in her stomach, a kind she hadn't felt since the morning she learned that her sister was murdered. She knew Marshall was dead—all that was left was the confirmation. She swallowed hard, but it felt like there was a blockage in her throat.

Looking up at the fluorescent lights, she focused on one that was flickering. The siren of an ambulance from the parking lot echoed throughout the lobby.

"Ma'am, if you can please have a seat and Doctor Coleman will find you. He should be down here shortly."

Hannah rested her forearms on the counter and glanced down at the woman's badge. "Please Alice, I just need to know if he is alive," she said with sincerity.

Alice caressed Hannah's hands. "I'm so sorry darling. He passed away about thirty minutes ago."

"Are you sure?"

She closed her eyes and nodded.

Hannah covered her mouth and started to hyperventilate. She spread her legs and clutched the counter, hands quivering.

"Not again," Hannah said, shaking her head. "This

can't be happening."

Alice stood up and motioned to another nurse.

"Honey, let me help you sit down. Mary, can you grab me a bottle of water?"

Hannah pulled her hands off the counter and stepped back. Her legs became weak like a sapling in a tornado. Glancing over her shoulder, she looked out the sliding glass door. It started to snow.

To hell with it. To hell with this life, to hell with everything. Hannah looked in her purse and stared at the gun. She closed her eyes and envisioned placing the barrel into her mouth and pulling the trigger. Her life would be over in mere seconds. No more death, no more life, no more sorrow, no more heartache, nothing.

She slid her finger onto the trigger and slowly exhaled.

The metal was cold against her skin, and she could almost taste it on her lips. She leaned her head back and embraced death. She thought she'd feel something. She didn't. She thought she'd be overcome with emotions. She wasn't. She thought she would cry. Not a single tear.

But, as much as she coveted the end, Hannah knew she'd also be killing her father. He couldn't bury another child, and he'd probably be dead before the funeral—best bet would be suicide by car off Lookout Mountain with a bottle of Vodka between his legs. She needed him as much as he needed her. They were each other's salvation.

She opened her eyes and stared blankly at the wall clock, watching the second hand tick life away. Alice said something, but Hannah couldn't comprehend the words. Then she heard a constant hum, like tinnitus. She was unsure if the sound was real, or a figment of her imagination.

After about ten seconds, she looked back to the nurse.

"Thank you for all your help," Hannah said.

She turned and started jogging toward the entrance.

"Ma'am, do you want to wait for Doctor Coleman?" Alice said. "Ma'am! Ma'am?"

Tom sat on the couch, feet on the coffee table, left hand holding a rocks glass half full of Jack Daniel's, the TV remote in his right. Max lay beside him, chin on Tom's thigh, faintly snoring.

Aimlessly he flipped through channels, briefly stopping on each one before pressing the up arrow.

Channel 4, local news, weather report, ten seconds. Channel 5, Pepsi commercial, five seconds. Channel 6, PBS, Frontline, fifteen seconds. Channel 7, local car dealership commercial, five seconds. Channel 9, local news—

"On Sunday morning, around 3 a.m., officers responded to a parking garage on the 1700 block of Market Street in downtown Denver on reports of a shooting. Once on scene, officers found an unidentified male with multiple gunshot wounds. The man was transported to Denver Health but later succumbed to his injuries. According to Denver police, this is Denver's twenty-third homicide this year—up 32 percent from the same time frame last year."

Tom pressed up, continuing the endless channel surfing.

Twenty minutes later, a series of knocks sounded at the door. Tom muted the television and glanced down at Max, the dog didn't hear a sound and continued sleeping.

"Tom, it's Claire."

Tom studied the door, unsure what to do. He sat still for a long moment.

"Please Tom, I heard the TV turn off so I know you're

home. Just open the door," Claire said, slamming on the door knocker.

"Stay, stay," Tom whispered to Max.

Tom got up and looked through the peephole. Claire was standing on the porch alone. He slowly opened the door.

"Hello, Claire."

"Hi, Tom. How are you doing?"

"You know, I have my good days and my bad days. Just one day at a time, you know. Yourself?"

"I'm good, thanks." She paused. "I've tried calling you a bunch of times, and left I don't know how many messages."

"I'm so sorry. I've been really bad about returning calls lately, and I never check my damn machine," Tom said, aloof.

Then there was a long, awkward silence.

Finally, Claire said, "Can I come in? It's freezing out here."

"Yes, yes, of course. Please come inside."

Tom ushered Claire in. They hugged, then he took her jacket and hung it on the coat rack. Max stared at her before burying his head under a pillow. Walking into the living room, they took a seat on the couch.

"Would you like a drink?" Tom said.

"Sure, I'll take a coffee or tea if you have it."

"I don't think I have either of those—it's been a couple weeks since I've been grocery shopping. I think all I can offer is water, expired milk, and a wide array of whiskey."

"Then I'll take whiskey with some ice."

"Easy enough."

Tom walked into the kitchen and started pouring the drink.

"What brings you up to my neck of the woods?" Tom said.

"I just wanted to make sure you're doing okay. I haven't heard from you since Lisa left, so I got a little worried."

"I appreciate that Claire, I really do, but you didn't have to drive all the way up here." He paused. "It's been hard, but I'm just trying to live one day at a time."

Tom returned to the living room and handed Claire the rocks glass, then sat on the couch between her and Max. She smiled and thanked him as they each sipped on their drink.

They talked about the Broncos winning the Super Bowl, President Clinton being acquitted by the Senate in his impeachment trial, the Colorado blizzard, and Claire's job as a high school art teacher.

There was a long silence, then Claire said, "I'm worried about you, Tom, I really am. I hate saying this, but you look horrible."

It'd been a long time since someone voiced concern about his well-being. It wasn't surprising because Claire was the compassionate one out of the sisters, and he always felt at ease talking to her.

Tom nodded. "Do you ever drive somewhere and when you get to where you're going, you don't remember the drive or how you got there? Like you don't remember changing lanes or making turns, or crossing intersections, or stopping at stop lights?" he said, sipping on the drink.

Claire silently nodded.

"That's my life. I don't know if I'm coming or going, asleep or awake, dead or alive. I'm just numb, numb to fucking everything."

"Jesus Tom, have you considered going back to the meetings, grief counseling, seeing a professional, fucking something? You can't live like this," Claire said.

"Those people don't know what I've lived through. They can't help me."

"Then let me help you, please," she said, placing her hand on his thigh. "I always hated the way Lisa treated you after everything that happened. It wasn't your fault or her fault, and neither of you could have prevented it. But Lisa needed someone to blame, and you were the scapegoat. She embraced the self-pity, and I don't know if she'll ever be able to get past it."

Tom stared into his glass, clinking the ice cubes.

"We live in a world where fucking horrible things happen, and that scares people, and some people want to turn and close their eyes to it, and they don't want to think something like this can happen to them, but it can, and it does."

She cleared her throat.

"You're a great man, Tom, and you did everything you could to find Megan, but Lisa, she—she was incapable of seeing that."

Claire slid her hand up his thigh, up his chest and onto his neck, pulling him toward her.

"Let me help," she whispered, inches from his earlobe.

"I don't think we should do this," Tom muttered.

"Please, I've dreamt about this for a very long time."

Tom started to speak, but Claire placed her index finger on his lips. She leaned in, and they both closed their eyes and kissed.

Suddenly Tom pulled back, placing his left hand on the cushion and his right hand, still holding the glass, on the armrest. It was the first time he'd felt the lips of another woman in almost two decades. It felt familiar, reassuring, and comforting.

Tom let go of the glass and slid his hand up her shirt, caressing her breasts over her lace bra. Claire climbed onto Tom, straddling him, kissing his neck.

She moaned and flung her left arm out, knocking the

glass off the armrest. It tumbled to the hardwood floor, shattering into countless pieces. Tom looked down at the shards and the pool of whiskey seeping into the cracks of the floor. Without warning, Claire grabbed his head and turned it back to her, placing her lips on his, easing her tongue into his mouth.

"Take me upstairs," Claire whispered, nibbling on his bottom lip.

Tom paused and thought about what was about to play out. They'd go upstairs, and have sex, on his and Lisa's bed, in his and Lisa's bedroom, in his and Lisa's house.

Tom pulled back and turned away. "I can't do this, Claire," he said. "I still love Lisa."

"I love her to death, but fuck her. She ran away and left you alone. Fucking alone, because she is too scared to face reality. And I'm here. Let me help fix you."

Tom looked down at the whiskey on the floor.

"I think you should leave," Tom said.

"Don't do this, Tom."

"Please Claire, you need to go."

Tom stood up and started up the stairs without turning back or uttering another word.

Hannah sat in a twelve-by-ten room with a metal table and three metal chairs and a single small window overlooking the Denver skyline. Across from her were two men, in their late thirties or early forties, who could have been mistaken for brothers. They introduced themselves as Detective Watkins and Detective Mann. Even the names were interchangeable.

She continually spun a red Bic lighter in circles on the table, not looking up from it.

"Can we get you a water, coffee, anything to drink?" Mann said.

Hannah looked up, first to Watkins, then Mann. She studied them for a few moments, then looked past them out the window to the ashen sky.

"No," Hannah said.

She lit a cigarette. Mann slid a white ceramic ashtray across the table.

"I'm sorry about Marshall. I know a bunch of guys that used to work with him, and they all said he was a damn good detective. Nothing but admiration for him. It's a shame whenever we lose one of our own, especially under these circumstances, and I promise you, we take it very personally," Watkins said.

Hannah nodded reluctantly. This was the last place she wanted to be.

"Do you know what Marshall was doing in that garage?" Mann said.

"I don't."

"Would you happen to know who he might have been meeting?" Watkins said.

"No, I sure fucking don't," she said, still spinning the lighter.

"Hannah, we are on your side, and we know you're hurting, and we want to catch whoever killed Marshall as bad as you do," Mann said.

"And being standoffish, providing non-answers, is not going to help us," Watkins said.

Hannah shrugged and listened to the silence in the room.

"Do you know who would've wanted to kill him?"

"He's been a cop or a PI for almost twenty-five years and put a lot of people in jail for a long time, so I'm sure there's a laundry list of people who wanted him dead," Hannah said.

Detective Mann opened a folder, removed an eight-by-ten printout, and slid it in front of Hannah.

"Have you ever seen him before?" Mann said.

Hannah glanced at the picture, then looked at the detectives and shook her head no.

"Well Hannah, that is Randy Hoffman, thirty-eight, of Denver, meth addict and a lifetime criminal—a real piece of shit if you ask me," Watkins said. "He's been in and out of jail most of his adult life, with his longest stretch being a five-year conviction for third degree assault down in the Springs, but his record includes drug convictions, B and E, aggravated motor vehicle theft, domestic violence, three DUIs, and hell, that's only the stuff he's been convicted of. I could keep talking about how much of a waste of life this guy is, but I think you get the point," Watkins said.

Mann tapped on the picture, "Look very closely, Hannah—have you ever seen this man before?"

"No, I sure haven't," Hannah said jamming the cigarette into the ashtray.

Shifting in the chair, she looked past Watkins and Mann and fixated on the Cash Register Building. If she could remember correctly, it was fifty stories. Her mind started to drift, wondering how long the fall would last if someone took a nose dive off the top story—a five, maybe ten-second free fall.

And maybe those mere seconds felt like a lifetime, an eternity. Your life flashing before your eyes, everyone you've ever met, everyone you've ever loved, every place you've been, and everything you've ever experienced from birth until that very moment of stepping off the ledge. Or maybe, just maybe, it'd be a few measly seconds of nothing, then splat.

Mann asked another question, but Hannah ignored him and lit another cigarette. Gradually she tilted her head back and blew the smoke toward the fluorescent lights.

Mann pounded his fist against the table. "Hannah, are you listening to me?"

"Yes. I'm fucking listening, but the issue is I don't give a fuck what either of you are saying."

"Well, would you like to know why we're asking about Randy?" Mann said.

"Do tell."

"We have two witnesses that saw a Suburban matching Randy's speed out of the parking garage moments after the gunshots. And one of them even matched the last three numbers of Randy's license plate," Mann said.

"And here's where the story gets compelling, Hannah," Watkins added. "A couple of hours ago, we found the Suburban four blocks south of the Coliseum, and Randy was in the driver seat with his neck slit ear to ear. Nearly decapitated. We also found a gun in the car, and I'm willing to bet my next paycheck that when we get the ballistics back on that, it'll match the gun to the bullet that killed Marshall."

Hannah turned and blew a puff of smoke, then cleared her throat. She had a strong feeling that Randy was an acquaintance of Nathan and Craig. He'd probably murdered Marshall in exchange for a large quantity of drugs, but instead of compensating him with the drugs, they killed him to tie up any loose ends.

"I wish I could help you guys, I really do."

"Why don't you enlighten us and tell us about any cases you've been working?" Watkins said.

"I highly doubt this is related to any of our current cases."

"Then it should be pretty easy to rule them out," Mann said.

"You know, the usual. Wives thinking their husbands are banging the secretary, insurance fraud, corporate surveillance. Nothing exciting."

"That's it?" Mann asked.

Watkins shook his head. "That's strange, because I've heard through the grapevine that you guys were working a missing girl case from Grand County. Megan Floyd? Does that ring any bells?"

Hannah paused and leaned back in the chair, attempting to gauge how much they knew about the investigation.

"Your boss was just murdered, so now is not the time to be lying to us," Watkins said.

"He was my friend, you fucking asshole. And yes, we were hired to investigate the Floyd disappearance," Hannah said.

"There we go. Maybe you should've led off with that one," Watkins said.

Hannah took a long drag. "I guess it slipped my mind."

"I'm sure it did," Watkins said.

"Have you guys had any new leads or breakthroughs? Anything?" Mann asked.

They had no clue about Nathan or Craig. They really were dumber than they looked.

"What do you think?"

"I'm asking because I don't know," Mann said.

"No, that case is as cold as they get," Hannah said.

"So, you've been working it for weeks and don't have anything new?"

Hannah smirked. "Half the cases you guys solve fall into your fucking lap, and the ones that take real investigation work, like the Floyd case, have zero leads after countless hours of police work. Not a fucking thing. We were starting from scratch, so how about you stop giving me shit."

"That wasn't our case. If it was, there'd be a different outcome," Mann said.

"Fuck you! Fuck both of you! I'm sure you would've had better luck than the CBI, the County Sheriff's Office and whoever else had their hands on this case," she said, twisting the cigarette into the ashtray.

Watkins glanced at Mann.

"I don't know Hannah, we're pretty good investigators," Watkins said.

"I don't know why the fuck I'm still here."

Mann cut in. "Because we're trying to figure out who murdered Marshall, and I'm positive it goes beyond that piece of shit meth head Randy Hoffmann."

"Can I go?"

"You have nothing to tell us about the Floyd case?" Watkins said.

"Can I fucking go?" Hannah said louder.

Watkins leaned into the table, stroking his chin.

"If we discover that you're withholding information or evidence or I find you've been lying to us, don't think I won't bring obstruction charges against you, because I will, and the next time you're back in this room it won't be so pleasant," Mann said.

Hannah vaulted out of the chair, pushing it back a couple of feet, nearly tipping it over.

"Fuck off. You don't intimidate me one bit," Hannah said, turning to the door, extending a middle finger behind her.

"I think we'll be talking again real soon, Hannah," Watkins said as she turned down the hallway.

It was 9:14, and Hannah had been in her car for almost

an hour without seeing any vehicles enter or leave the parking lot, and no sign of anyone in or around the building or the adjacent one. If someone was watching her, they were invisible. She decided to wait five more minutes.

Hannah gently closed the car door, not making a sound, then flung on her backpack and jogged down the alley to the back of the building. She unlocked the door, opened it, walked up a flight of stairs, and rested her ear against the second-floor door. Nothing. She eyed her Beretta for a long moment, then placed her hand on the doorknob, turned it, and pulled the door back. Anxiously, she opened it three inches and peered into the hallway. Empty. She slid through the opening, then tiptoed across the carpet until she arrived at the second door on the right.

Hannah stared at the plaque attached to the door: *Marshall York - Private Investigator.* Slowly, she moved her fingers over the lettering.

Pulling out her keys, she unlocked the door, slipped into the office, and locked it in a single graceful motion. Then she slid down the door to a crouching position, elbows between knees, palms over her face. She remained still for a long time. The realization that she was never going to see Marshall finally hit her at that moment, and it put her on the verge of a nervous breakdown. She wanted to lie on the floor forever but was confident that if she didn't solve his murder, it'd never get solved. Now was not the time to mourn—that would come after those bastards were dead or behind bars.

Leaning into the door, she slowly got up, then crept down the hallway in the dark to Marshall's office. Hannah walked over to the desk and sat down on the office chair. It was the first time she'd ever sat in Marshall's chair, and she briefly thought about standing or sitting on the floor, but it felt reassuring so she remained seated.

With ease, she pried open the top middle drawer and removed a black address book. She flipped through the pages, stopping on the S's. Tracing her finger down the page, she started tapping a number with her index finger. Finally, she picked up the phone and dialed.

"Hello," a voice said.

"May I speak to Sara?" Hannah said.

"This is she."

Hannah cleared her throat. "Sara, my name is Hannah Jacobs, and I'm an associate at your father's private investigation firm."

Dead silence. Hannah paused, searching for words.

"Why are you calling me about Marshall?" Sara said, her voice cold.

Hannah bit down onto her lip.

"Well, I don't know how to say this, and I'm so sorry, but your father was shot and killed last night."

A long pause. Then Sara spoke. "I'm sorry your boss died, but Marshall ceased being my father fourteen years ago when he decided to walk out on me and my mother. He made his decision to leave us, and I made my decision to disown him as my father, and I've been content with the arrangement for some time. And if I'm being honest, I'm not going to shed a tear for some guy that destroyed his family because life got too hard for him."

Hannah wanted to tell her that Marshall was a good man, and that he missed her and loved her, but she knew it wouldn't matter. Sara hated Marshall with the same intensity that Hannah hated her mother.

"I just—just thought you should know that he's dead."

"What was your name again?"

"Hannah."

"Well Hannah, I don't know your relationship with Marshall, and I honestly don't care, but to me, Marshall died a long time ago. He walked out of my life when I was fifteen, a fucking teenager. And I cried for almost a year, wishing he'd come home, but he didn't, and I vowed to myself I'd never shed another tear over him."

"I'm sorry for bothering you," Hannah said gravely.

"Oh, and please don't call my mother—I can promise that she'll care less than I do."

Sara hung up before Hannah could respond. Defeated, she dropped the handset onto the desk, causing a loud bang that startled her even though she knew it was coming. She leaned over and spit into the trash can, then watched the spit slither down the transparent bag.

Once the spit disappeared, she opened the bottom drawer and removed a half-empty bottle of Jim Beam. Without hesitation, she put her lips on the bottle and drank three large gulps. After gagging, the whiskey started to warm her stomach and a feeling of relaxation overcame her. She stretched her arms back then picked up the phone and made her second call of the night.

"Hello?"

"Is this Tom Floyd?" Hannah said.

"Yes it is, who is this?"

"My name is Hannah Jacobs—I'm an assistant of Marshall York." She paused, realizing she'd used the present tense. "I think we need to talk."

An hour later, Hannah was leaning against her car, parked on a dirt road eight miles west of Denver. Looking up at the moonless sky there were no clouds and very little light pollution. She couldn't remember the last time she'd seen the stars so luminous. She traced her finger along Ursa Minor and Cepheus.

The night was cold. One of the coldest nights in weeks,

probably in the low twenties. She hated the cold, and dreamt of the day she'd live on a beach. A long way from Colorado and all of the memories.

Sometime later, a rabbit bounced over the gravel and stopped about five feet in front of Hannah. The animal looked at her, ears pointing straight to the sky. Then it vanished into the overgrown vegetation as quickly as it had appeared.

Headlights approached from the east. Hannah stood up and watched the beams bounce across the gravel road. The vehicle was somewhere around two hundred feet out, probably driving around thirty-five. A giant dust cloud formed behind it.

She lumbered to the middle of the road, watching the headlights flicker on the horizon. The engine roared as the vehicle got closer, and closer, and closer while her heart beat faster and faster.

"Don't freak out, it's gotta be Tom," she whispered under her breath.

At about fifty feet, the vehicle started to slow, and at twenty feet she could make out the vehicle and see the silhouette of a driver and passenger. It was not Tom's 4Runner. It was a third-generation Ford Bronco, with a rusted hood, a rusted side panel, and a deafening engine. The dust cloud stretched almost a quarter of a mile behind it.

Hannah stepped back, slid her hand inside her jacket, and wrapped her fingers around the grip of her gun.

The Bronco slowed as it approached Hannah. A man stuck a hand out the window and started to wave. She watched, then lifted her chin, swallowing hard. It stopped in the middle of the road, about ten feet directly in front of her. Clouds of black exhaust poured out the tailpipe, and the air smelled of gasoline and brake pads.

"Have you seen a dog running around here?"

"A dog?" Hannah yelled, barely over the engine.

"Yeah, a Black Lab. She jumped my fence like an hour ago, and I can't find the little bastard."

She stared at him for a moment, then released the gun and pulled her hand out of the jacket.

"No, I haven't seen any dog," she said.

"Well, if you do see her, her name is Daisy, she's super friendly. And my number is on the collar, so I'd appreciate it if you gave me a call if you do find her," the driver said.

Hannah nodded. The man smiled back, and then the Bronco sped off. Within thirty seconds, the taillights disappeared into the night.

About twenty minutes later, Tom came in from the same direction, and without introducing herself, she told him about Marshall and the meeting in the garage, and how he was shot and bled out for almost an hour until a parking attendant found him, and that he died the previous night, and about Detective Mann and Detective Watkins, and then about Nathan and Craig, and finally she told Tom that she'd found Megan's Chevy Blazer in the barn on Lone Peak.

Realizing she hadn't allowed him to respond, she stopped and waited for Tom to say something, but he remained silent.

Finally, barely audible, he said, "Take me to her car."

An hour later, Hannah slammed on the brakes at the turnout for the barn. Stupefied, she stared at the ruins of the structure. Only one support beam was still erect, hovering above the piles and piles of charred wood and ash. A scattering of bright red embers gleamed in the debris.

"They fucking burned it," Hannah said with a nervous laugh.

Disappointment coursed through her entire body. The crowning achievement of her career was reduced to ashes.

They exited the car and walked in silence to the smoldering remnants of the barn.

"I have a strong suspicion we're never going to see that car again," Hannah said.

"We're getting close, and they know it," Tom said.

Hannah nodded, then kicked a clump of dirt into the fire. They stared at the ashes and listened to the remaining embers for a few minutes, then started walking back to the car.

"So, what's our next move?" Tom said.

Hannah was surprised by the question, but then remembered without Marshall, she was the lead investigator on the case. Hell, without Marshall, she was in charge of the entire PI firm. She wasn't sure if she was ready for that type of responsibility, but she didn't have a choice.

"I need to go have a talk with someone. I'll give you a call in the morning with an update."

"Do you want me to go with you? A little backup never hurt anyone."

For a moment, she considered the offer, but there was no need for both of them to be in harm's way.

"No, no, I'll be fine. It should be a simple conversation."

"Okay," Tom said, nodding.

"What are you going to do?"

"Go where I've been almost every night for the last week—the Black Bear Inn."

"Please try not to get yourself killed," Hannah said, and before she finished, she felt bad for saying it.

They stood in the middle of the dirt road, both of them speechless. It wasn't an awkward silence, just two strangers sharing a common bond, striving for the same goal.

Hannah opened her arms and hugged Tom hard. She wasn't a hugger, but she sensed he needed the touch of another person.

"I promise we are going to find her," she whispered.

Later that night, Hannah climbed up the fire escape, pried open her kitchen window, then slid across the countertop and onto the floor. She remained still in the dark for ten, maybe twenty seconds listening. Finally, the silence was broken by Milo's purring.

"Come here, sweetie," she whispered, making kissing sounds.

Kneeling, she pet Milo, massaging under his neck, then picked him up, kissed his head, and set him back on the tile. She tiptoed down the hall to her bedroom, knelt, reached under the bed, and removed a tattered leather suitcase. Popping the latches, she opened it and smiled.

Tom had been in the Black Bear parking lot for almost two hours, and he wasn't sure how much longer he could stay awake. The adrenaline of finding Megan's car was quickly depleting. He grabbed a coffee out of the cup holder, took a sip, then leaned back into the headrest. The caffeine wasn't working.

About thirty minutes later, his eyes slowly closed, and he gradually slipped into a light sleep. Eventually, he was startled awake by a figure standing in the middle of the lot, about twenty feet directly in front of him. The shadow cast down across the parking lot like a giant.

Tom rubbed his eyes, and the man quickly came into

focus. It was the face in the picture that Larry had given him. It was the face he saw every time he closed his eyes. It was Nathan.

They watched each other for a tense moment. Then Nathan gestured for Tom to roll down the window. Tom stared back before tentatively turning the crank.

"I hear you've been looking for me!" Nathan shouted.

Tom was motionless. He'd obsessed about this exact moment for the last two years, and now that it'd finally become a reality, he was unsure what to do.

"Come on, let's go have a drink and chat," Nathan said, gesturing to the bar.

Nathan casually strolled across the lot toward the entrance. Tom reached for his gun and briefly contemplated putting a round in him. At that distance, he was somewhat confident he could shoot to wound, a bullet to the thigh or the back of the kneecap, incapacitating enough to gain control and question Nathan on his terms, but if that bullet pierced the femoral artery, he could bleed out within minutes, and any possibility of finding Megan would also die along with him in that parking lot.

He slipped the gun into his belt and opened the car door.

Tom knew he could be walking into a trap, but he didn't care. This was the closest he'd come to solving Megan's disappearance, and he might not get another opportunity to confront the man who killed her. He'd sacrifice his life for answers about what happened.

Cautiously, he walked across the parking lot and into the bar. He stood in the doorway, looking from left to right. There were eight men and one woman, the bartender, visible inside the bar. The bartender was behind the bar reading a newspaper. Three drunks sat at the bar top, each separated by two stools. Three more were playing pool, and another man was sitting in a booth watching SportsCenter. Nathan was sitting at a high-top in the middle of the bar. "Back Home Again" by John Denver echoed throughout the room.

"Tommy Floyd, please take a seat," Nathan said, gesturing to a stool across from him.

Tom stared for a moment, then walked to the table and sat directly across from the monster.

"Lucky Strike?" Nathan said, offering him a cigarette.

Tom glanced at the cigarettes, then gave a slight shake of his head.

Nathan lit a cigarette. "Well, it's nice to finally meet you. I've heard a lot about you, mostly good," he said with a large smile. "And I can see in your eyes that you want to jump across this table and rip my fucking head off, but I strongly suggest you don't do anything stupid. I wouldn't want you to get hurt tonight. I'm just here to talk."

Tom remained still. Nathan looked behind him and gestured to the bartender.

"Hey sweetheart, what do we need to do to get a couple of drinks?"

The bartender looked up for five seconds, then back down to the paper.

"Fuck man, I remember walking into this place and within five minutes I'd have a drink in my hand and a shot down my throat. Well, not anymore—this chick would rather read her horoscope than help the customers. I'm telling you, good customer service has gone the way of the buffalo, like everything else in this world."

Nathan looked back to the bartender but quickly turned to Tom again.

"What do you drink? I'm thinking whiskey, probably a middle-shelf American bourbon like Jack Daniel's or

Jim Beam. Am I right? I'm betting you're a Jack and Coke type of guy."

"Coors Light," Tom muttered.

"Well fuck, I was completely wrong. I guess this round is on me. Sugar tits, can we get a Coors Light, a PBR, and a shot of Jameson?" Nathan shouted.

He opened his wallet and placed $20 on the table. Tom's eyes momentarily wandered to the "Free Beer Tomorrow" sign behind the bar surrounded by softball and bowling trophies.

"Yeah, yeah. One sec," the bartender said, barely audible.

The room was quiet for a moment, then "Layla" by Derek and the Dominos started playing. Nathan took a drag and looked up at a speaker hanging from the corner of the bar.

"Do you know the story behind this song?" Nathan said.

"Yeah, Eric Clapton wrote it as a love song to Pattie Boyd, who was married to George Harrison at the time."

"Fuck man, everyone knows that. Do you know about James Gordon, the drummer of Derek and the Dominos?"

"No, I don't."

Nathan ran his fingers through his greasy, slicked-back hair and licked his lips.

"Well, James Gordon was the drummer on "Layla," but he also wrote and recorded the piano outro. I mean, that is probably one of the most recognized piano parts in the history of rock and roll." He paused for a moment and listened to the song. "Here's the thing that most people don't know—James was an undiagnosed schizophrenic."

The bartender dropped off the drinks, grabbed the $20, and walked away without saying a word.

"The change is all yours, sweetheart," Nathan called

after her before returning to his story. "Well, one night, James showed up at his mother's apartment, and when she answered, he hit her with a hammer, then proceeded to stab his mother with an eight-inch butcher knife until she was dead. He murdered her right in the hallway of her own fucking apartment. And do you know what his motive was?"

Tom remained still, lips clenched.

"He said the voices told him to do it. The voices."

"Why the fuck are you telling me this?" Tom said.

"Hold up, this is the best part," Nathan said, whistling the piano melody, weaving his hands around his head like a conductor. Then without warning, he brought his hands down, took the shot and slammed the glass down on the table. "I'm telling you because sometimes you never know who is fucking insane until it's too late."

"You don't fucking scare me."

"I should! And Tom, I'm being honest with you, I really am. I think you should get back into your car and drive back to your nice little house up in Granby and never, ever ask about me or my doings, or say my name to another person again. Shit, to be on the safe side, I'd suggest staying the fuck out of Evergreen altogether."

"The only way I'll stop is when I find Megan."

"I consider us friends, so I'm going to tell you a secret. If someone really wanted to dispose of a body up in the mountains, that body would never be found unless said person told someone where to look. And my guess is that if you're the type of person that'd bury a body in the mountains, you're not going to tell anyone where to look."

"I know you burned the barn. I know you moved Megan's car. You know I'm getting close," Tom said, slamming his fists onto the table, spilling beer out of the nearly full pint glass.

Nathan smiled gravely, then glanced at his watch.

"Well Tom, it's been a lovely chat, but I really have to get going. And my condolences about Marshall."

"You go to hell, you piece of shit!" Tom said, jumping off the barstool. He reached for the gun in his belt.

"I wouldn't do that if I were you," Nathan said, motioning to the booth behind Tom.

Tom turned around. The man who'd been watching SportsCenter when he walked in was pointing a gun directly at him. Tom watched the man for a moment, then turned back to Nathan.

"If you shoot me, he will shoot you. And he is very accurate at this range. Precise," Nathan said.

Tom stared, dead-eyed.

"And who are we kidding, anyways? We both know you wouldn't shoot me, because without me, you have no chance of finding your precious Megan. Nada," Nathan said, making a zero with his fingers.

He was right. As bad as Tom wanted to put a bullet in Nathan's head, he couldn't. Not without getting answers about Megan.

"I'm never going to stop looking for her."

"I'm leaving now, and please take my advice and stay out of Evergreen, because it'll be best for your long-term well-being. I can promise you—if we meet again, I will not be as cordial."

Nathan knocked twice on the table, then stood up and began strutting to the door. Seconds later he began whistling the piano coda to "Layla."

Frozen, Tom watched Nathan and the man with the gun walk away, unsure if he'd ever have the opportunity to confront Nathan again.

Before exiting the bar, Nathan paused and turned

around. He smiled then slipped out and into the darkness. The man stood at the door for another thirty seconds, maybe a minute, then steadily backed out with the gun still aimed at Tom.

The moment the door closed, Tom raced to the exit, and as he reached the parking lot, a Ford Ranger turned west onto Morrison, tires squealing. As he approached the 4Runner, he noticed the front driver-side tire was nearly flat. At the tire, he bent down and saw numerous punctures in the sidewall.

"Fuck, fuck, fuck!" Tom yelled, punching the tire.

Standing between Craig's house and a juniper bush, Hannah peered through the living room window, watching Craig as he sat at the kitchen table flipping through the pages of a *Hustler* while sipping on a beer. He studied each page like he was preparing for a college exam.

The night was quiet, calming her nerves. She wondered if she'd ever become accustomed to situations like this. Probably not, but that didn't mean she wasn't up for the challenge.

Glancing at her watch, she deemed it was now or never. After a deep breath, she ducked under the window and stepped onto the front porch. She pressed the doorbell, took a step back, and raised her arm, waiting for the door to open.

"Get the fuck off my porch!" Craig shouted from inside.

Without hesitation, she rapidly pressed the doorbell four times in succession.

"I told you to get the fuck off my property, you stupid motherfucker!"

Boots on a wood floor sounded from inside the house. They got louder, and louder, and louder. Then the chain unlatched, and the deadbolt turned, and the door flung open.

Craig and Hannah stared at each other for a second before she stuck a cattle prod into his lower abdomen and pulled the trigger. There was a loud buzzing sound as the two metal tips emitted twenty thousand volts throughout his body. He dropped like a stone onto the floor.

Hannah rushed into the house, slammed the door, and jabbed the tips of the cattle prod into his inner right thigh. She smiled, then pulled the trigger for a second time. He wailed as his limbs flailed. After about ten seconds, Hannah released the trigger. Craig looked up at her wide-eyed, tears gushing down his face. Then he mumbled something incoherent. She was confident he was incapacitated.

"I can't tell you how valuable it is to know a guy who's a whiz with electronics. For a hundred bucks, he modified this little thing to send out four times the voltage."

Then she hovered the cattle prod over his groin. Craig flinched, preparing for the shock, but she didn't pull the trigger. As much as Hannah wanted to kill him for his involvement in Marshall's murder, she couldn't. If she did, she'd be no better than the degenerates and criminals she pursued.

"It puts out one hell of a stinger, doesn't it? You'll be lucky if your dick works after tonight," she said with a smile.

"Fuck you, you little fucking cunt!" he slurred.

"I find that word repulsive, so I dare you, call me the c-word again. I double dare you."

"You stupid cunt!"

"You're really dumb," Hannah said.

At once she jammed the prod into his groin and pressed the trigger.

"Stop! Please stop!" Craig screamed, spewing saliva.

She released the trigger after ten seconds, then looked down at him, her face blank.

"I wouldn't want to be in your position right now, I really wouldn't."

"I don't keep any money in the house," Craig muttered.

"I'm not here to rob you."

"Then what the fuck do you want?"

"Answers," she said.

Across the living room, Katie eyed the handgun on the end table, about seven feet directly in front of her. She began calculating the odds of reaching the gun and pulling the trigger before Nathan could react.

In her drug-fueled life, she'd fired countless times at beer cans in Nathan's backyard. She was a decent shot, hitting about half the cans at forty feet. Holding a gun felt comfortable, and she knew if she could reach the table, he'd be dead, and everything would be over, but that was a big if.

The gun could be a ploy to test her devotion to Nathan. She could see him placing the unloaded weapon on the table, within striking distance, to see if she'd try to make a dash for it. If that was the case, she probably wouldn't see another morning. Katie stared at the weapon for a long time, then dropped her head in defeat.

"I should've just fucking killed him! What the fuck was I thinking? This would be over and I'd never have to hear her fucking name again!" Nathan yelled.

Katie glanced up at Nathan, and he eyeballed her with

closed fists. She slithered back into the wall on the cold, hardwood floor. Her legs trembling, heart hammering, lips clenched, concentrating on every breath.

Nathan began pacing the living room, mumbling something while counting with his fingers. Katie sat still, watching him ping-pong across the room. After about a minute he stopped, turned to her, and crouched down, straddling her outstretched legs. She closed her eyes and braced herself to be hit.

"Look at me sweetie," Nathan whispered.

She slightly opened her left eye. Hovering inches from her face, he was motionless, expressionless, lifeless.

"You're going to make another call for me."

Katie swallowed hard. "No, I won't."

"I'm sorry, but you really don't have a say in the matter," Nathan said, slowly fondling her left cheek.

Then his hand slid over her chin until his fingers were wrapped around her neck. The grip became tighter, and tighter and tighter. Katie was fighting for every breath.

If she didn't make the call, she knew he'd continue to squeeze his hands around her neck until she was dead. By making the call, she might merely be extending the inevitable, but at least she'd live to see another day.

"I'll make the call," she whispered.

"Good."

Nathan released the grip, then slowly ran his hand up her face and began wiping away the tears.

"Come on, get up."

Instantaneously, he grabbed her bicep and sprang up, pulling her with him like a ragdoll, then dragged her across the floor and into the kitchen. Pulling out a chair, he dropped her into it and took a seat next to her.

From his pocket, he removed a folded piece of paper and dropped it on the table. Glancing down at it she became queasy. It was Tom's number, on the piece of paper he'd handed to her before she left his house.

For a long moment, she stared at the phone number, attempting to devise a plan. The first thought was to tell Tom that it was a trap the moment he answered. That'd save Tom, but Nathan would hang up before she could reveal any crucial information, and that would most certainly be her demise. The next thought was to insert clues in the conversation, but the odds of Tom understanding without Nathan figuring out were extremely low. Then she thought of a plan that had the highest probability of saving Tom, and herself.

Nathan instructed Katie on what to say on the call and then made her repeat it three times.

"Are you ready?" Nathan said.

She nodded reluctantly.

As Nathan turned on the cordless phone and started to dial, Katie glanced down at the paper and began memorizing the phone number—*four three four, seven nine, seven five*, over and over and over, trying to cement the digits into memory.

"Now please don't do anything stupid," Nathan said, dropping a polaroid on the table.

Katie looked at the picture and instantly averted her eyes. It was Megan, in a shallow grave with her throat slashed from ear to ear. She became very afraid, her heart racing like a marathon runner.

Nathan pressed the call button, then handed the handset to Katie. She placed it against her ear and looked down at the paper. Reaching across the table, Nathan grabbed a second cordless phone and turned it on, ready to listen to her every word.

The phone rang three times before a brief silence.

"Hello," Tom said.

"Tom, it's Katie. I'm sorry, were you sleeping?"

"No, I'm awake. Is everything okay?" Tom said.

"Yeah, I'm fine. Thank you."

"I've been worried about you, so that's good to hear. Did you make it to Nebraska?"

"No, I'm actually in Denver, but plan on leaving in the next few hours." She paused. "And the reason I'm calling is that when I was packing, I found a journal that belonged to Megan. It was in this backpack that I haven't touched in years. I have no idea how it got in there."

"Did you read it?"

"No. The moment I saw her handwriting, I shut it. I couldn't read her journal."

"Can I come pick it up? Tom said.

"Of course. If you're available tonight I can meet you, or else I can mail it when I get to Nebraska."

"Tonight. You tell me when and where."

"How about Bear Creek Park off of 285 and Sheridan at about two-fifteen?"

"I'll be there," Tom said.

They said goodbye and ended the call.

"Very good job," Nathan said.

Out of the corner of her eye, she saw a fist coming at her. She attempted to avoid it, but it was too late. The punch landed on her temple, knocking her out of the chair and onto the floor.

When she opened her eyes, she was lying on the couch with Nathan hovering over her. He stared back at her with an evil smirk, reminiscent of Ted Bundy. Chills ran down her entire body.

Her head was throbbing, she was dizzy, and her vision was blurry. She wasn't sure how long she'd been unconscious—five minutes, maybe ten. She'd had a concussion at fourteen after a car accident nearly ejected her out the front windshield, and she was almost certain Nathan had just given her a second one.

Suddenly, he grabbed her ankles and began wrapping duct tape around the cuffs of her jeans, completing probably five rotations.

"Give me your hands," Nathan said.

Katie obeyed, holding them above her stomach. Nathan completed two rotations around her wrists, tore the tape, and tossed the roll behind him. Putting his thumb and index finger on the outer parts of her lips, he forced a smile. Then, without saying a word, he turned and started up the stairs.

Katie closed her eyes and remained still. On an endless loop, she repeated the phone number—*four three four, seven nine, seven five.*

About five minutes later, Nathan returned wearing a backpack. "I should be back shortly. Please be a good girl."

Barely audible, Katie said, "I promise I will."

Nathan turned and slowly walked out of the living room, then out of sight. A few moments later, the front door slammed, the deadbolt turned, and the house was silent again. Katie lay rigid for a long time, staring into the TV screen reflection, watching the world through the living room window.

"Four three four, seven nine, seven five. Four three four, seven nine, seven five," she whispered.

EIGHT

I n a slow, rhythmic, steady tempo Katie repeated the
phone number, over and over and over, envisioning
it written down on the piece of paper.

She eyed the digital clock on the VCR—it displayed 1:44.
Nathan had been gone for twenty-five minutes, and she
was confident that he wasn't coming back to check on her.

Rocking against the couch, she wobbled her body until
she was in a sitting position, with her feet on the floor
and her hands in her lap. She moved her wrists back and
forth inside the tape, struggling for almost five minutes,
but there was little give.

Lifting her hands around her chest, she brought her
elbows together, then slammed them down around her
rib cage. A small rip appeared in the tape.

With all her strength, she raised her hands, pulled
her elbows together, and slammed her arms down again,
this time with more force, causing the tape to rip apart.
She separated her arms and stared at the torn tape on
both wrists.

"Holy fucking shit!" she said.

After ripping off the tape, she sat up and untied her shoes and kicked them off. Then she unzipped her jeans, sliding them down inside out until they reached her ankles and the tape. She swayed, stretching the tape, inching her feet through the tight opening. After about thirty seconds, her ankles were free, and she kicked the pants off and onto the floor.

Katie sprang off the couch and searched the room for a phone, but there was nothing. She turned and sprinted into the kitchen, tripping over herself in the hallway, falling into the wall and hitting her head. After regaining her balance, she continued down the hall.

In the kitchen, she tore a piece of paper off a magnet notepad on the refrigerator and frantically searched for something to write with. She yanked open one drawer, then another, and on her third attempt, she found the junk drawer. A ziplock baggie of pens, markers and pencils was at the front of the drawer. She grabbed the baggie, pulled out a pen, and scribbled on the notepad until ink appeared. Then she scrawled down the number.

Completely exhausted, she dropped her elbows onto the counter, trying to catch her breath. Drops of blood trickled from her right wrist onto the laminate countertop in a growing pool.

On the wall was the cordless phone docking station, but the phone was gone. She yelled some obscenities, then ran upstairs into the master bedroom. Frantically she searched the room, pulling the sheets off, looking under the bed, pulling open every drawer on the dresser, but nothing. Then she ran to the second bedroom, where there was another docking station on the nightstand, but that cordless phone was also missing. She pressed the handset paging button, and nothing. At that moment, she realized Nathan had taken all of the handsets.

"Fuck!" she screamed.

Katie ran back downstairs, grabbed her pants and shoes, then headed back into the kitchen. Opening the junk drawer, she removed a pair of scissors and cut open the tape. After it was off her pants, she scrounged the junk drawer for change, finding four dimes and three nickels. Enough for two phone calls.

She slid her pants on, then her shoes, barely tying them as she started running toward the front door. As she passed the dining room table, she spotted the polaroid out of the corner of her eye. She grabbed the picture, slipped it into her back pocket, then continued to the front door.

At the door she hesitated, envisioning Nathan on the other side. After a silent prayer, she placed her hand on the doorknob and turned.

The patio was empty, the driveway was empty, and the night was dark and still. She took a long, deep breath then started sprinting up the gravel driveway.

Tom veered onto the 285 off-ramp, turned on the blinker, then slowed to a stop at the Sheridan Boulevard intersection. The street was deserted, and he briefly considered running the red light, but decided against it. Leaning back, he anxiously began drumming on the steering wheel in rhythm with the blinker.

He knew the meeting could be a trap. Marshall had been baited into an ambush, so if it worked once for them, why not reuse the same game plan? But what if it wasn't? What if Katie actually had Megan's journal and there was something in it that implicated Nathan? It could be all he needed to end this nightmare.

At the top of the driveway, Katie looked to the left, then the right, then the left again. Mountains surrounded her in every direction. After a moment, she took one step to the left, then shifted her entire body to the right and started sprinting due east, leaving tiny dust clouds with every step.

Ten minutes into her run, Katie hadn't seen a single car, or person, or house, or business. Nothing but mountains, trees, and street signs. She felt more alone than she'd ever felt in her entire life.

Exhausted and weak, she slowed to a stop and placed her hands on her knees, trying to catch her breath and keep her balance. She didn't want to stop, but she began to vomit, mostly liquid, onto the pavement. Her legs and lungs were on fire, her feet were numb, her side was cramping, and she was dizzy.

With every step, she thought she'd collapse, but she knew she couldn't give up, and after a long minute, she looked up and pushed herself off her knees and continued toward the never-ending horizon.

About twenty minutes after Katie started east on the desolate road, she saw the glimmering lights of a Texaco gas station sign. The interior lights were off, and there wasn't a single car in the parking lot, but there was a payphone next to the building.

Tom turned into Bear Creek Park and stopped at the entrance. Soccer fields to the left, 285 above to the right, and in the distance, he could see Katie's Corolla in the parking lot about two hundred yards straight ahead. He rolled down the window and extended his arm outside the car, feeling the cool, crisp air. He watched the car for a minute, then slowly started toward the parking lot.

Tom pulled into the parking spot next to the Corolla and turned off his headlights and engine.

"Katie," he said.

After a few moments, he called her name a little louder. Nothing but the howling wind. He surveyed the parking lot, the park, the playground, and the restroom. Nothing.

Tom stepped out of the 4Runner and cupped his hands on the passenger window, peering in. An empty pack of Lucky Strikes sat in the center console. Suddenly he remembered Katie smoked Marlboro Reds and Nathan smoked Lucky Strikes. He turned to the front of the car, then cautiously stood up, placing his hand on the gun in his belt.

He took a heavy step forward, then another, then another. Then stopped and listened, his eyes traveling east to west, west to east, over and over and over.

Katie stumbled as she approached the payphone but caught herself on the plexiglass of the booth. She held on to it for a few long moments, worried that her legs would give out and she'd drop to the pavement. After a deep breath, she slid three dimes into the phone slot and dialed.

Leaning into the handset, she glanced up at the sky and wiped away tears with the back of her hand. Seconds later, the line connected and started ringing.

"God damn it Tom, please fucking answer!" she screamed.

Tom's Nokia 5110 chimed across the parking lot. As he reached for the phone he saw a muzzle flash and heard a crack, followed by the whiz of the bullet inches from his head. He instantly lunged to the ground, crashing hard into the pavement, smashing the cell phone in his front pocket.

Another muzzle flash and another crack. The bullet ricocheted off the hood of the Corolla and into the windshield, shattering the glass. Shards flew into the air, raining down on his body and the parking lot.

Tom reached back and pulled his gun out in front of him. He shuffled across the pavement, the glass crushing under his jacket with every movement. Then he steadied his hands, aimed at the brick building, exhaled, and fired one round.

The bullet from Tom's gun hit the corner of the building, and fragments of brick exploded in all directions.

From across the parking lot, Nathan screamed, "You motherfucker, I'm going to kill you! You hear that? I'm going to fucking kill you!"

Two more rounds came from the building. Both of them whizzed above Tom at about fifteen feet.

After the shots, the night was quiet except for cars on the highway. Tom watched the building, patiently waiting for any movement, any shadow, any signs of life, but there was nothing. He became confident that he'd wounded Nathan, either with a bullet or pieces of shrapnel. He'd wait another few minutes, then clamber to get a better angle.

Then, like a rabbit, Nathan sprang up and started sprinting away on the sidewalk. Tom jumped to his feet and commenced the pursuit.

Katie hung up, pulled the piece of paper out of her pocket, and stared at it. It was the number she remembered, and the number she'd dialed. She tried it again, but the phone rang and rang and rang. Staring blankly at the number pad, she pressed the hook switch down and released it, waiting for a dial tone before pressing three numbers.

"911 what is your emergency?" the operator said.

"My name is Katie Harper, and I've been kidnapped and held hostage by Nathan Cook." She paused, but before the operator could respond, she blurted while reaching for the polaroid, "I also have evidence that he murdered Megan Floyd."

Tom sprinted across the sidewalk past the playground with a swing set, monkey bars, and the giant concrete sombrero that doubled as a slide. He was faster than Nathan and getting closer and closer. Fifty feet, thirty feet, twenty feet.

Nathan leapt off the sidewalk, onto a dirt slope that led to a creek. A few steps down the slope, Nathan tripped and tumbled down the hill. In the fall, his gun was dislodged, coming to a rest at the edge of the creek.

Tom carefully navigated the hill and reached Nathan before he could get back up.

"Don't fucking move," Tom said.

He trained the gun at the back of Nathan's skull. Then he stood for a long time, watching the man lying face down in the dirt. Finally, he sidestepped around Nathan and started toward the creek, maintaining his aim. He picked up Nathan's gun, cleared the chamber, and slid it into his belt. Walking back, Tom stopped about five feet in front of him.

Nathan looked up, his face plastered with dirt and blood. A splinter-sized piece of brick was protruding out of his right eye and a two-inch stream of snot dangled out of his right nostril. Nathan pinched his left nostril and blew the snot into the dirt.

"You know all of this is your fault," he said.

"Get up! And don't say another word," Tom said, gesturing with the barrel of the gun.

"You don't even realize it, man," Nathan smirked. "This, Megan, and everything that has happened between that night and right now is your fucking fault."

Tom didn't want to be alone with Nathan. Not because he was scared of him, but because he was scared of what he might do. He knew the more Nathan spoke, the easier it would be to kill him.

"Shut the fuck up and get up!"

"If it wasn't for you, your little Megan would still be here."

Nathan started rolling in the dirt, sending a pine cone skittering toward Tom. He kicked it into the underbrush.

"If you don't shut up, I'm going to break your fucking face!"

"Shit man—after all this time, you still don't know why."

"What the fuck are you talking about?"

Tom knelt, aligning the barrel parallel with Nathan's forehead.

"You, fucking you! Your badge, your job. It's all because of you!"

Tom shifted uneasily.

"You killed Megan because of me? Because I was a cop?" he said, his voice cracking.

"Ding, ding, ding! Johnny, show him his prize behind door number one," Nathan said, pounding his fists onto the dirt.

In disbelief, Tom felt the world closing in on him. It was his fault that Megan was dead. If he had been an accountant, or a car salesman, or a fucking janitor, she'd still be alive. But he was a cop, and that was the catalyst of her demise.

"No, no, no!" Tom said, shaking his head.

"Yes, yes, yes. She was running shit for me, and I was informed that her daddy was a fucking cop. A fucking cop? So yeah, I had to take care of her. She was a fucking liability."

Tom sprung up and rushed forward, then pulled his right foot back and kicked Nathan square in the mouth with the toe of his boot. It was the hardest he'd ever kicked anyone or anything, and he was certain he'd broken some bones and shattered some teeth.

Nathan remained still for about ten seconds, then slowly lifted his head, attempting to hide his pain. A steady spray of blood trickled out of his mouth, down his throat, soaking his shirt. He reached to his mouth, wiped the blood off his teeth, then grabbed his front tooth, wiggled it a few times, and swiftly ripped it out. He stared at the tooth for a moment, then tossed it over his shoulder.

"Roll the fuck over," Tom yelled.

Nathan groaned, then slowly rolled onto his back.

"Where is Megan?"

"I'll never tell you."

"Tell me, or I swear to God I will kill you right now," Tom said through clenched teeth.

Nathan glared at Tom, then slowly began shaking his

head. Tom got an uneasy feeling that he was looking into the eyes of a dead man.

Methodically, Tom raised the gun and aimed it at Nathan's chest. With a look of fear, Nathan turned away. Tom slid his finger over the cold, curved metal and exhaled.

"Stop, Tom! Stop!"

Tom glanced up to see Hannah standing at the top of the slope. She stood still for a second, then steadily side-stepped down the hill.

"You'll never find Megan if you kill him!" Hannah yelled, almost out of breath. "She'll never be at peace."

"He killed Megan. He fucking killed her!" Tom said.

Staring at her, expressionless, tears began running down his face.

Hannah cleared her throat. "I know he did, but I promise, you don't want it to end like this."

Tom remained very still, breathing through his nose.

"You know if you pull that trigger, everything you've been searching for will die with him." She paused. "Please, give me the gun."

"I don't know if I can," Tom said, barely audible.

"We have him, and we'll get a confession. I promise we'll find her. You just have to trust me," Hannah said, placing a hand on Tom's shoulder.

Tom peered up at Hannah then quickly back to Nathan.

"Please, give me the gun," she said, extending her hand.

Tom was motionless for a long time. After what felt like minutes, he extended his arm and offered the gun to Hannah. She quickly grabbed the weapon from him and said something, but he didn't hear her. It was as if everything had gone silent. Then, almost in slow motion, he turned and walked to the creek. He looked up to the sky and the clouds, and the crescent moon and the stars, and started to wipe away the tears.

Two months later, while Tom was packing, the phone rang. He placed the tape on top of a U-Haul box and answered the phone.

"Hello."

"Tom, this is Detective Mann. I'm calling to give you an update on the investigation. Nathan took a plea deal." He paused. "And in exchange for not pursuing the death penalty, he pleaded guilty to Megan's murder." He paused again, this time longer, probably waiting for Tom to say something. Finally, Mann continued. "Life in prison without the possibility of parole. Also, part of the deal stated he'd have to disclose the location of Megan's body. And I'm so sorry to tell you that we discovered her remains in a shallow grave about five hundred yards behind the Cook family house."

"Are you sure it's Megan?" Tom asked.

"There was identification in the grave that belonged to Megan, and the clothing matched what she was last seen in. Forensics is confident that the remains will be identified as her. I'm truly sorry, Tom."

Tom was speechless. He'd known this call would come one day, but hearing the confirmation that Megan was officially gone was heart-wrenching.

When Megan wasn't found after the first week, he was almost certain she was dead, but he always had a tiny sliver of hope that she'd be found alive. That sliver was now gone. But Megan being found was an ending, a chapter of his life that he could close. And with that chapter closed, it gave him the chance to piece his life back together.

"Tom, you still with me?" Mann said.

"Yes, sorry."

There was another five minutes of conversation about the plea deal and the investigation, but Tom wasn't cognizant of anything being said. He was thinking about Megan, and how happy she seemed on the last day he saw her. That was how he wanted to remember her.

Tom thanked Mann for the call and hung up. He remained still for a long time. He thought about that night by the creek. If Hannah hadn't arrived that night, he would've killed Nathan, and Megan would've never been found.

Hannah sat at the kitchen table, sipping on coffee while a mix CD was playing in the background. Songs off of Fugazi's *13 Songs*, Beck's *Odelay*, Jane's Addiction's *Ritual de lo habitual*, Refused's *The Shape of Punk to Come*, and Radiohead's *The Bends* were heavily featured on the disc. The bass line of "Waiting Room" by Fugazi began playing.

While staring out the window, she thought about cutting herself for the first time in a long time. It wasn't that she wanted to do it, it was that she couldn't remember the last time she'd had the urge, or even thought about doing it. It'd been almost eighty-one days since she sliced her thighs after the motel room with Benjamin. Solving the Megan Floyd case provided her with a feeling she'd never had before, a feeling of self-worth, and it gave her hope for the future.

Hannah grabbed a two-inch stack of mail, then pulled the trash can next to the table. She started tossing most of the mail into the trash and created a new pile for bills or anything that looked important.

About halfway into the stack, there was an envelope addressed from her mother. She stopped and flicked the corner with her index finger. Finally, she tore it open and removed a birthday card. The cover was an illustrated cake with candles and the words "Happy Birthday" in big, bold, colorful print. Hannah opened it, and two twenty-dollar bills fell onto the table. Two short sentences were written in the card, ending with *Take care, Mom.*

Without reading the entire inscription, Hannah closed the card and tossed it in the trash. Then she picked up the twenty-dollar bills and ripped them in half, then ripped those pieces in half, then did it one more time. She dropped the torn pieces and watched them rain into the trash. In her eyes, the only parent she had left was her father.

Hannah finished sorting the rest of the mail, placed the trash can under the sink, and walked into her room. She opened her closet and rummaged through items on the top shelf, removing a three-ring binder. Lying on the bed, she gazed at the picture of her sister taped on the cover. Hannah pulled the binder up to her face, kissed the picture, then set it back down on the bed and opened the binder. This was the only case that mattered to Hannah, and the one that she'd solve or die trying.

Pulling into a gas station, Katie climbed out of her car and started pumping gas. As she was stretching, an old man walked past her on the other side of the pump.

"Excuse me, sir, do you know how much longer until Merriman?"

"You got about another two, two and a half hours of nothing on 61," the old man said, pointing north.

Katie looked east at the flat, featureless horizon, then

looked back to the man and smiled.

"Perfect. Thank you."

As Hannah walked up Broadway, she spotted Tom on a park bench across from the capital. He stood up as she got close, and they hugged and greeted each other.

"I'm guessing you heard about Nathan?" Hannah said.

"Yeah."

"At least that bastard is going to die in jail."

"I'm not going to lie and say I wish he wasn't dead, but I guess this is the second-best outcome," Tom said.

"Fingers crossed he gets shivved in the shower," Hannah said with a smile.

Tom crossed his fingers and waved them in front of his face.

"And I've got to give it to you and Marshall, I didn't think she'd ever be found, and I sure as shit didn't think you guys would be the ones to solve it," Tom said.

"I honestly didn't think we would either."

They both laughed, then leaned back on the bench and remained silent, watching cars drive by.

After a while, Tom said, "I never did ask how you knew I was going to be at the park that night."

"Let's just say applying high voltage directly on a guy's testicles will get him to say almost anything."

"Enough said." Tom smiled. "I guess the only thing left is your payment."

Reaching into his pocket, he pulled out a check and handed it to Hannah. She looked at the amount, $25,000, rubbing the ink like it would change or disappear. For someone who lived paycheck to paycheck, this was life-changing.

"What is this?" she said.

"That is what Marshall and I agreed on—including the bonus if Megan was found."

"No, I can't take this," Hannah said, offering it back to Tom.

"You deserve every penny of that check as much as Marshall, so please, put it in your purse and go to your bank and cash it."

Hannah thanked Tom numerous times, and then they made small talk for a few minutes.

"Shit, I need to get going," she said, looking at her watch. "I got a lunch date with my pops, and I don't want to be late."

They hugged and said their goodbyes, then Hannah got up and started walking away.

"Hannah, I couldn't have found Megan without you and Marshall. You saved me that night, and I'll always be grateful for that," Tom said.

She smiled and nodded, then turned and started down the sidewalk, avoiding the cracks.

From the cemetery, Tom glanced up to the Rocky Mountains, becoming hypnotized by the snow-covered peaks along the Continental Divide—Apache Peak, Mount Audubon, Copeland Mountain, and Longs Peak.

Tom knelt and positioned a bouquet in front of the gravestone, then ran his fingers across the surface, back and forth, up and down, over and over and over again. After a long sigh, he leaned in and kissed the impala-black granite. Megan was finally at rest.

Later that day, Tom closed the front door behind him for the final time and strolled down the driveway with Max in tow. About halfway down, he stopped and looked at the For Sale sign in the front yard.

An old man driving a rusted Dodge truck slowed to a stop in front of the driveway. He rolled down the window.

"You moving, Tom?" the old man said.

"Yeah, the house should be on the market sometime this week."

"Well, that's a shame. I'm going to miss seeing you and the wife around town."

"Thanks, Arthur. I'm going to miss it here as well, but it's time to move on."

The old man nodded. "Where are you going?"

"California," Tom said.

On a trail outside of Evergreen, Hannah inspected each passing tree, searching for what she deemed a perfect trunk. A mile into the hike, she stepped off the trail and approached an Aspen. She unzipped her backpack and removed a pocket knife. Extending the blade, she started carving into the smooth, white surface, "RIP Marshall." She took a step back to admire her work. With a quick smile, she turned and continued down the trail.

At the lake shore, she dropped her backpack onto the sand. She stretched her arms above her head, then looked down at the capillary waves at her feet. She splashed the water, soaking her hiking boots.

Taking a seat on a small boulder, she removed a note from her backpack. Carefully, she unfolded the paper and stared at the writing with unfocused eyes, looking through it to the lake and the sun setting behind the ridge.

Finally, she focused her eyes on the writing.

Hannah, if you are reading this, I must have really fucked up. I really hope it was a fiery car crash or a bear attack and I didn't OD on the toilet like Elvis. You know I've never been one for words, so I'm going to keep this short. I just want you to know I love you like a daughter, and you gave me a second chance at something I fucked up, and I love you for that. I know you're going to solve Casey's murder. It'll get tough, and you're going to run into countless dead ends, and you'll think it will never be solved, but you're a talented investigator. Don't ever forget that. Don't ever doubt yourself, just keep working the case, and the leads, and the evidence, and eventually you'll find who did it. I know you will. Keep smiling and shining bright. Love, Marshall

She slipped the note back into the backpack, then pulled out a small glass vial. She stared at the ashes inside for almost twenty minutes, crying, then smiling, then crying again. Hannah wasn't sure if the pain would ever go away, but she didn't want it to. The pain reminded her about Marshall.

Pushing on the boulder she stood up and brought the vial to her lips, kissing it countless times. After one last kiss, she flung it out over the lake. It produced a small splash before quickly disappearing under the surface. She watched the water for a few minutes.

Freely, she jumped off the boulder, then pressed play on her Discman. The opening guitar riff of "Rebel Rebel" by David Bowie blared in her headphones. Music made everything right in the world.

Turning back, she started up the path, stopping after a couple of steps to pick a columbine. She brought the flower to her nose, sniffed the petals, then placed it behind her right ear. Hannah turned back to the lake and watched the sun fade behind the mountaintops before turning and continuing up the trail.